BLANK CONFESSION

ALSO BY PETE HAUTMAN

All-In

Rash

Invisible

Godless

Winner of the National Book Award

Sweetblood

No Limit

Mr. Was

BLANK CONFESSION

PETE HAUTMAN

SIMON & SCHUSTER BFYR

New York   London   Toronto   Sydney   New Delhi

SIMON & SCHUSTER BFYR

An imprint of Simon & Schuster Children's Publishing Division
1230 Avenue of the Americas, New York, New York 10020

SIMON & SCHUSTER BFYR is a trademark of Simon & Schuster, Inc.
For information about special discounts for bulk purchases, please contact
Simon & Schuster Special Sales at 1-866-506-1949 or
business@simonandschuster.com.
The Simon & Schuster Speakers Bureau can bring authors to your live
event. For more information or to book an event, contact the
Simon & Schuster Speakers Bureau at 1-866-248-3049 or visit our website
at www.simonspeakers.com.
Also available in a SIMON & SCHUSTER BFYR hardcover edition
Book design by Krista Vossen
The text for this book is set in Melior.
Manufactured in the United States of America
First SIMON & SCHUSTER BFYR paperback edition November 2011
6 8 10 9 7 5
The Library of Congress has cataloged the hardcover edition as follows:
Hautman, Pete. 1952—
Blank confession / Pete Hautman.
1st ed.
p. cm.
Summary: A new and enigmatic student named Shayne appears at high
school one day, befriends the smallest boy in the school, and takes on a noto-
rious drug dealer before turning himself in to the police for killing someone.
ISBN 978-1-4169-1327-6 (hc)
[1. Drug dealers—Fiction. 2. Bullies—Fiction. 3. Conduct of life—Fiction.
4. High schools—Fiction. 5. Schools—Fiction.] 1. Title.
PZ7.H2887 Bl 2010
[Fic] 22
2009050169
ISBN 978-1-4169-1328-3 (pbk)
ISBN 978-1-4424-3638-1 (eBook)

ACKNOWLEDGMENTS

Thank you to Swati Avasthi, H. M. Bouwman, K. J. Erickson, Leslie Harris, Ellen Hart, Mary Logue, and Virginia Lowell for their many helpful suggestions, and to Jack Schaefer for providing the map.

Five lousy minutes.

Detective George Rawls hung up the phone, brought his feet down from his cluttered desktop, looked at his watch, and sighed. If the kid had walked into the station five minutes later, Rawls's shift would have been over. He would have been driving home to enjoy a peaceful dinner with his wife.

Five more minutes and Benson would have caught this case. Rawls stood up and looked over the divider toward Rick Benson's desk. Benson, looking back at him, smirked. Rawls rolled his eyes and hitched up his pants. They kept falling down—his wife's fault, all those vegetables she'd been feeding him since his cholesterol numbers came in high.

He opened the upper left-hand drawer of his desk and took out his service revolver. Rawls was old school; he still used the weapon that had been issued to him as a rookie. He emptied the cylinder into the drawer and slid the unloaded weapon into his shoulder holster.

The unloaded gun was a prop. These young punks were impressed by such things. Most of them. He left his jacket hanging on the back of his chair and made his way out of the room and down the hallway toward the front entrance. He walked past the long citizens' bench, automatically checking out the four people sitting there: A slight, pale-faced boy—black jeans, black T-shirt, scuffed-up black cowboy boots—sat with his elbows resting on his knees, staring at the floor. Probably some middle-school bad boy picked up for shoplifting. Next was a young woman wearing a tight skirt, smeared mascara, and a nasty bruise on her right cheek. A hooker, no doubt. Then an anxious-looking older woman, probably there to report a runaway husband, or a purse snatching. At the end was a scowling middle-aged man in a rumpled suit—could be anything.

Rawls made these assessments automatically and effortlessly. Part of the job.

Directly facing the front doors of the police station, John Kramoski sat behind his elevated desk flipping through the duty roster. Rawls stopped in front of him. The desk sergeant looked up.

"Sorry, George," Kramoski said. "I know your shift is almost over, but you were up. And it's a kid—your specialty."

Rawls was the precinct's unofficial "Youth Crimes" officer. He had once believed that, working with kids, he might actually make a difference. These days he wasn't so sure.

"Where is he?" he asked.

Kramoski jerked his thumb toward the bench.

Rawls looked over, surprised. "How come he's not in the interview room?"

"He walked in here by himself. Besides, look at him. What's he gonna do?"

"We're talking about the kid on the end, right?"

"Yep."

Rawls shook his head. "He looks, like, twelve."

"Says he's sixteen."

"Jesus."

"And Mary and Joseph, bro." Kramoski returned his attention to the duty roster.

Rawls walked back down the hall, past the man in the suit, past the older woman, past the prostitute. He stopped in front of the kid and waited for him to look up. It took a few seconds. The kid's hair was thick, the color of dried leaves, maybe three weeks past needing a cut. He slowly sat back and raised his head to look directly into Rawls's eyes, his expression devoid of all emotion.

Rawls felt something throb deep within his gut. He had seen that expression before, on other faces. The face of a mother who had lost her only child. The face of a man who had just learned he would be spending the rest of his life in prison. The face of a girl who woke up to find that she would never walk again. A look of despair so deep and profound . . . it was as if the connections between the mind and the face were severed, leaving only a terrible blankness.

He had seen that expression in other places too. The morgue. Funeral parlors. Murder scenes.

The face of the dead.

But this boy was not dead. Somewhere behind those eyes there existed a spark—a spark that had brought him here, to this building, to this bench, to George Rawls.

"Are you Shayne?" Rawls asked.

The boy dropped his chin. Rawls took that as a yes and sat beside him on the bench, feeling every last one of his forty-three years, fifteen of them as a cop. Despite having conducted hundreds of such interviews, he found himself at a loss. Something about this kid—who could not have weighed much more than his Labrador retriever—frightened him. Not fear for himself. The other kind of fear: fear that the universe no longer made sense, that everything was about to change.

"So . . . ," Rawls cleared his throat, looking straight ahead, ". . . who did you kill?"

2. MIKEY

I met Shayne the same day I got busted for having drugs in my locker, which was also the day after this huge thunderstorm that knocked over a bunch of trees, including the giant elm in our backyard.

I was walking to school. I had left home early so I could look at the storm damage. I could hear chain saws from every direction. Each block had three or four trees down. Some had fallen on houses, some against power lines, and there was even one big oak tree completely blocking Thirty-first Street.

None of the buses had arrived yet when I got to the school. As I started up the wide, shallow steps leading to the front door I heard a humming, burbling sound and looked back to see a motorcycle pull up to the curb. A battered BMW, at least thirty years old. The tank and fenders were painted primer gray. The seat was patched with duct tape. The rider, dressed in a black T-shirt and black jeans, put down the kickstand and took off his helmet.

My first thought: *He looks too young to have a driver's license.*

He ran his fingers through his hair, hung his helmet

on the mirror, looked at me, looked at the school, looked back at me.

"Nice suit," he said. He had a soft, crisp voice, and some kind of accent.

"Thanks." I was wearing my dark gray three-button, the one with the cuffed trousers. "Nice bike," I said. I can be a little sarcastic sometimes.

He looked down at his battered motorcycle. "Not really." He gestured at the school building. "You go here?"

"Why else would I be here?"

He nodded. "Me too. I just moved here. I start today. Where's the student parking?" Definitely an accent—maybe southern, but with a sharp edge to it.

"See that sign?" I pointed. "That huge sign that says STUDENT PARKING?"

"Oh," he said.

Once again looking at my suit, he said, "Is there, like, a dress code or something?"

I took in his frayed T-shirt, his holey jeans, his beat-up black cowboy boots. "Lucky for you, no. As long as you don't wear gang colors or a T-shirt with swear words."

He nodded. "So what's with the suit?" He didn't ask it meanly, just in a mildly curious way.

"Some people like to dress nice," I said.

He nodded as if he understood, popped the helmet back on his head, turned the bike around, and rode off toward the parking lot.

I didn't even know his name, but already I liked him.

Mi nombre es Miguel Martín, and no, I am not Mexican. Actually, I am Haitian on my mom's side. Her parents came from Haiti back in 1971. They speak Haitian French. I am learning Spanish, however. My mom wanted me to learn French, but learning Spanish is more useful on account of I am often mistaken for Mexican, even by Mexicans, which is weird because Pépé—Mom's dad—is black. That deep purple-black skin color that comes from the west coast of Africa via Haiti. My grandmother, Mémé, is freckled, red-headed, and white. Her ancestors sailed to Haiti from France back in the 1600s. That's her story, anyway. These days her red hair is from a dye bottle, but she claims it's her real color.

My mom turned out to be a medium-brown-skinned woman with Afro hair that turns reddish in the summer. My dad is white, third or fourth generation Italian American.

Anyway, when all those genes got mixed up, I somehow came out looking Mexican. Imagine a Mexican kid, kind of small, wearing a suit and oversize tortoiseshell glasses. That's me. My sister, Marie—we're in the same grade even though she's ten months older than me—has light skin and our grandma's freckles, but her features are more African-looking.

My real name is Mike Martin, aka Mikey the Munchkin, and a *bueno día* is any day I don't feel the need to slink, or, in *español*, *escabullirse*. Do you know about slinking? It's a way of moving from place to place so people don't notice you. Cats are very good at it. Rats are even better. Lions and polar bears never slink. Okay, maybe a little, but only when they're sneaking up on you.

I have noticed that most short guys (I am the shortest guy in the eleventh grade) adopt one of two strategies. Some, like Chris Rock, or Prince, or Napoleon, have these enormous, noisy egos and make up for their lack of size by dressing and talking big. Others just try not to get stepped on. This is also true of small dogs, which tend to be either world-class barkers or world-class slinkers.

I do it all. I dress big, I bark, and I slink.

I *escabullirse*d into American Lit class and took my usual seat near the windows a few seconds before the 7:40 chime. A few minutes later, the kid with the BMW walked in. Mr. Clemens gave him a raised-eyebrow look.

"Sorry I'm late, sir," he said. "My name is Shayne. With a *Y*. Shayne Blank. I just transferred here."

Mr. Clemens, startled by all his politeness, directed Shayne-with-a-*Y* Blank to the empty desk next to me.

Here's what was weird. Every one of us had our eyes on him, the way we would stare at any new face, but this kid appeared to be perfectly comfortable, relaxed, confident, and alert. I've met cats that could pull that off—that combination of hyperalertness and megaconfidence—but I'd never seen it in a human. So, after class, being a friendly and inquisitive type of guy, I followed him into the hall and introduced myself properly. We went through the whole where-are-you-from-what-are-you-doing-here routine—he told me he was originally from Fartlick, Idaho, and that his dad was on a secret mission to Afghanistan, and that his mom was in the Witness Protection Program, and he was living with his aunt.

"I suppose she's an astronaut or something," I said.

"Yes. But from another planet."

I liked his sense of humor.

"I thought maybe you were from the South. Because of your accent."

"I have no accent," he said, in an accent.

"So is Blank your real name? Or an alias?"

He frowned. "You don't like it?"

I was opening my mouth to say something back to him when I felt a hand clamp down on my shoulder.

"Hey, Mikey."

"Hey, Jon," I said, trying to act as if I was glad to see him.

Jon Brande was borderline movie star handsome, with blond hair, sparkly blue eyes, a strong chin, and a toothpaste-ad smile—the picture of a vibrant, healthy teenager, ready to graduate with honors, accept a basketball scholarship to a Big Ten university, and go on to enjoy a brilliant career in politics. Except that Jon had been kicked off the basketball team his sophomore year and his grades were just barely passing.

Also, he was a violent, psychotic, drug-dealing creep.

"Listen." He hung his arm around my shoulders and turned me so our backs were to Shayne. "You got room for this in your backpack?" He handed me a brown paper lunch bag. It was limp and wrinkled, as if it had been opened and closed several times. "Just hold it for me. I'll get it back from you after school."

All my alarm bells were going off, but there was no way I could refuse. Jon was big, he was a senior, and he scared the crap out of me. I took the bag. I didn't have to ask him what was in it, but I couldn't help asking, "Why?"

"No reason." He winked and walked off.

Believe me, it is very creepy to get winked at by Jon Brande.

Shayne said, "Friend of yours?"

"Not really." I stuffed the paper bag into my backpack. "He's my sister's boyfriend."

On the way to the interview room, Rawls noticed that the kid was limping. The right leg of his jeans was dark and stiff below his knee. Dried blood? It was hard to tell with those black jeans.

"Hurt yourself?" Rawls asked.

"I'm okay."

"In here. Have a seat."

The kid limped around the table and sat down. Rawls left the door standing open. Some suspects were more forthcoming if they didn't feel trapped—it made them think they were there by choice, that they had some say in their immediate future. Also, Rawls preferred the door open because the room reeked. Years of citizens with poor hygiene and fear-sweat had permeated the gray-green walls. It got repainted every couple years, but the smell never really went away.

Rawls let the kid settle himself, then said, "Now, there's something you don't see too often."

The kid looked around, then met Rawls's eyes with a silent question mark.

Rawls smiled—he had been told he had a friendly

smile—and sat down. He let a few seconds pass, then said, "Your shirt."

The kid looked down at his T-shirt, then back at Rawls.

"It's a T-shirt."

"Yes it is," said Rawls.

"What's weird about it?"

Rawls waited a few more seconds to see if the kid would say more. He didn't. Rawls raised the kid's toughness quotient by a degree or two. Most people had a hard time not filling a silence.

Rawls said, "What's *weird* is, it's blank. No rock band, no logo, no message, no nothing." Rawls once again gave the kid room to respond, with no result. He said, "I didn't even know they made the things in plain."

The kid nodded, as if to say, *Okay, I get it. Next?*

Rawls pulled out his small blue notebook, set it on the table, and flipped through it until he came to a blank page. He clicked his ballpoint pen.

"How about we start with your full name."

"Shayne Blank."

"*B-L-A-N-K?*"

"Yeah. And Shayne with a *Y*."

Rawls wrote that down. "Address?"

The kid gave him an address on the west side, an okay neighborhood bordering one of the wealthier suburbs. Rawls wrote it down.

"Parents?"

"Yes."

"Two of 'em?"

"Three."

Rawls waited for clarification. The kid made him wait a few beats, then said, "Dad, mom, aunt."

"Who do you live with?"

"Aunt."

"What about your parents?"

"My dad's a SEAL."

"A navy SEAL?"

"No, the kind you see at the zoo."

Rawls sat back and regarded the kid, whose face remained empty.

"Are you sure you want to be making jokes, son?" Rawls said.

The kid shrugged.

"Where's your dad now?"

"Iraq. I think."

"And your mom?"

"Fort Story. That's in Virginia."

"Military brat, huh?"

The kid just looked at him.

"And your aunt? What does she do?"

"Nothing. She's retired."

"Who did you kill?"

The kid didn't say anything, same as the first time Rawls had asked him that question—instead, he reached for the metal ring attached to a hinge bolted to the tabletop and ran his fingers over it. The ring was there so that a potentially violent suspect could be handcuffed to the steel table, which was bolted to the floor. Rawls sat back and looked at his watch: 5:09. It didn't matter. This time he was going to wait for the kid to speak, no matter how long it took.

It took two minutes and thirteen seconds. The kid flopped the ring back and forth: Clank. Clank. Clank.

"It's kind of a long story," the kid said.

"You want something to drink? A soda?"

"No thanks." He was back to playing with the ring. "I just—" Clank. Clank. He took a deep breath. "You ever kill anybody?" he asked.

Rawls said, "No, I never killed anybody."

"You'd feel bad if you did, though. Right?" The kid looked up. Once again, Rawls perceived something steely and sharp behind the curtain.

"I suppose it would depend on the circumstances," Rawls said.

The kid took that in, nodded.

"Why don't you tell me what happened," said Rawls.

The kid said, "Okay. I just moved here, and—"

"From where?" Rawls interrupted him.

"I was in Louisville for a while."

"You get in trouble in Louisville?"

"Do you want me to tell you what happened or not?"

Rawls sat back in his chair and peeked at his watch: 5:14. If he couldn't wrap this up in half an hour, he'd have to call home and tell his wife to eat dinner without him.

"Go ahead," he said with a sigh. "Take your time."

I am not a guy who sticks his nose in anybody else's business, and I certainly did not want to get on the wrong side of Jon Brande, so I figured I'd hang on to his bag of whatever, give it back to him after school, and be done with it. I should have known better.

Several weeks earlier, a junior named Leon Sullivan OD'd on something—the rumor mill said it was ecstasy mixed with LSD but, knowing Leon, it could have been anything. He had climbed onto the top of the school in the middle of the day and announced his intention to fly. It took two fire trucks and half a dozen cops to drag him off that roof. Leon never came back to school. I heard his parents sent him to some boarding school for druggies.

I happened to know that Leon got the stuff—whatever it was—from Jon, but Leon never told anybody, so why should I? I may have a big mouth but I'm not suicidal.

Anyway, after Leon's monumental freak-out, the antidrug task force moved into high gear. We had special educational visits from narcotics detectives, antidrug movies, a big display in the front lobby with all sorts of drug information pamphlets and brochures, and even an antidrug "rally" in the gym, which was basically a nondenominational invocation by the youth pastor from Trinity Lutheran, and a stupendously lame exhibition by the cheerleading squad. Then came an invitation for all of us to come forward and pledge to remain drug free during our tender high school years. Out of the twelve hundred students at the rally, I think they got maybe thirty pledges, two of whom were hard-core stoners who goofed their way through the entire pledge. I'm pretty sure they were high at the time. There probably would have been more pledgers, but it was last period and the bell rang and the gym emptied in about one minute flat.

Jon thought the whole thing was hilarious. As the primary supplier to the local stoner population, he knew exactly how many students were using drugs, and how much they were using, and how many of them were unlikely to quit using, no matter how many rallies and pledges and invocations they were exposed to. His customer base was well-established and recession-proof. The only thing that could seriously mess it up would be if he got arrested and thrown in jail.

I should make it clear here and now that I was not one of Jon's customers. I'd tried marijuana once with Marie, but I didn't like it much. Besides, that stuff is expensive.

Also—don't laugh—I was one of the students who took the pledge.

The rest of the day—the day Jon gave me the mysterious paper bag—as I *escabullirse*d from one class to the next, I didn't think much about Shayne. My mind was more occupied with the bag in my backpack. I had this creepy feeling that something bad was going to happen, and I was right: Five minutes into the last period of the day, the principal's voice came booming over the PA system telling everybody to report to the gymnasium.

We all filed out of our classrooms like good little drones. I overheard a couple of guys saying something about a locker search. Like everybody else, I did an instant mental inventory of my locker. Nothing to worry about, except—uh-oh—was it against the rules to have Advil? Because I did have a bottle of headache pills in my locker.

We were almost to the gym when I heard a dog bark. At first I thought, *That's weird, a dog in the school* . . . then I realized what it was. Not just a dog, but a *drug sniffing* dog! And there I was with a paper bag containing who-knows-what stuffed in my backpack.

I quick ducked into a lavatory, dug the bag out of my backpack, stuffed it deep into the trash can, then rejoined the march of the drones. The dogs never came into the gym—they were strictly on locker duty. For the next hour, we listened to a very bored cop deliver a very boring lecture on the dangers of using illicit drugs, while four other cops checked every one of the 1,300 lockers lining the halls.

The official tally? They found a one-hit pipe in Gregg Houghton's locker, a minibottle of Jägermeister in Brandon Sayle's, some herbal diet pills in Yasmine Leach's, and my bottle of Advil. I think the cops were a little disappointed.

"Maybe if you tear through the back of my locker you'll find an opium den," I said.

I thought that was pretty funny, but the cop I was talking to was not amused. All four of us all got hauled to the office and searched. Gregg had a little bit of something in a twist of foil in the back pocket of his jeans. The cops arrested him on the spot. The rest of us, they just called our parents. I was hugely relieved, congratulating myself on my quick thinking getting rid of Jon Brande's paper bag, and not too worried about the Advil thing. My parents would think it was ridiculous, even though it was technically against the rules.

I didn't see Jon that day—my parents took me straight home. Fortunately, they were more pissed at the school than at me.

"Imagine that. Advil against the rules!" my mom said, shaking her head.

"They don't make rules so you can break them," my dad said, which made no sense whatsoever.

I went out to the backyard to sit in the gazebo and watch the tree service guys cut up and remove our fallen tree. Yesterday it had been a beautiful towering elm, but the storm had snapped it off about six feet above the ground, revealing the inside to be hollow and rotten.

My dad came out several times to offer suggestions to the tree guys. Dad was an engineer. He believed there was a right and a wrong way to do everything. I could tell he was kind of driving them crazy.

After another hour or so the tree was gone. They had cut the stump down to a foot above the ground. Dad stood out there staring at that stump for a long time. I supposed he was trying to figure out how to get rid of it.

But that was his problem. My problem was Jon Brande. The next morning, first thing, I went to the lavatory where I'd dumped Jon's bag, but the janitor had taken care of that. The trash can was empty.

"I started school the day after I moved here," said Shayne. "I'd switched schools before so it was no big deal. The idea was I'd stay here with my aunt and finish up the year here, then move back with my mom in the summer, and then maybe come back in the fall for my senior year."

"Why?" Rawls asked.

The kid shrugged. "I just go where I'm wanted."

Rawls nodded. Another kid whose parents didn't have time for him.

"You know Jon Brande?" the kid asked.

Rawls, keeping his face carefully expressionless, nodded. "I know Jon."

"How good do you know him?"

"Well enough." Rawls had had a few run-ins with Jon, but had never been able to make an arrest. "Is that who you killed?"

The kid suddenly became fascinated by his fingernails. "I met this kid named Mikey Martin my first day at school."

"A friend of Jon's?"

"Not exactly. Mikey's okay. Only he's one of these guys, he says whatever comes into his head, you know? His mouth gets him in trouble." He stared down at the steel ring on the table. "He can be real irritating sometimes."

"Is he a little Mexican kid?" Rawls asked, remembering. "Wears a suit?"

"Yeah. Only he's not Mexican."

Rawls grunted, thinking of the smart-ass kid in the suit and tie who'd had the bottle of headache pills in his locker during the antidrug blitz at Wellstone High—the kid had sure *looked* Mexican.

"I know who you mean," he said.

"We got to be friends, sort of, me and Mikey. That's how I met Jon."

Five hundred dollars.

That was what Jon Brande said I owed for losing his bag.

My big mouth said, "Is that retail, replacement cost, or just some number you made up?"

I saw it coming and had a fraction of a second to regret what my mouth had done before Jon Brande's fist smashed into it. My head snapped back and hit the side of the Dumpster, my glasses went flying off my head, and I sank down into a cushy heap of garbage. I was surrounded by torn-open trash bags. Bags I had pulled out of the Dumpster, ripped open, and rummaged through. It was disgusting—you can't even believe the stuff that gets thrown in the trash in school. I found everything from I-don't-want-to-think-about-it, to you-don't-want-to-know—but I did not find Jon's little brown bag.

"Five hundred dollars," Jon repeated.

"I don't have it," my smashed-up mouth said.

"Get it." Jon turned his back and walked away. I managed to keep my big mouth shut. It took me ten minutes to find my glasses—they'd landed in the emptied Dumpster.

Later, when I got home, I told my mom my mouth had

run into a door. She gave me a look, like she knew it was no door, but she really didn't want to know. My mom had run into a couple of doors herself back before my dad quit drinking. But for the past few years, everything had been cool at home, at least as far as my parents were concerned.

Anyway, I still had this problem, which was that Jon Brande had decided that I owed him five hundred dollars, and I didn't have it, or anything close to it. With nothing to lose, I talked to my sister.

Marie was perched in front of her vanity staring at the mirror.

"Jon is going to kill me," I said.

She said, "So?"

My sister. I don't know what she saw in the mirror, but here's what I saw: a light-skinned, freckled girl with African features, straightened hair dyed jet black (its natural color was more like chocolate brown with a little bit of red), too much black eye makeup, and dark red lipstick that always found its way onto her teeth. Not that she smiled much.

I said, "So my funeral will probably be, like, next Friday."

"That's my hair straightening appointment," she said.

My sister. To her, life was a really boring movie. None of it real.

"I was hoping you could, you know, *talk* to him?"

She plucked an eyebrow hair. Her eyebrows were plucked to thin arcs, like they'd been sliced into her forehead with a razor.

"He said you stole his inventory," she said. She pronounced it like *INNNNN-ven-tory*.

My sister.

"I didn't steal anything. He handed me this bag, and . . ." I explained to her what had happened, and how it wasn't my fault, and how now Jon expected me to pay him all this money I didn't have.

Marie stared at me as if I'd been speaking Klingon.

She said, "Well, don't look at me. I don't have it either." Then she went back to tweezing her eyebrows.

My sister.

7. THE INTERVIEW ROOM

"Every school I've been to, there's been a Jon Brande," the kid said.

Rawls nodded. It was true. He had run into more than his share.

"I try to avoid them," the kid said. He kept flipping the steel ring back and forth. Clank. Clank. It was driving Rawls nuts.

"You sure you don't want a Coke or something?" Give the kid something else to do with his hands.

"I'll take an orange soda if you got it."

Rawls left the interview room and walked down the hall to the soda machine. No orange soda. He bought a Mountain Dew. Maybe the caffeine would make the kid talk faster. On the way back he stopped and phoned home to say he would be late.

"Some kid walked in to confess to a murder," he told his wife. "I'm still trying to figure out who he thinks he killed."

"I hope you like cold fish," she said.

"What kind of fish?"

"Cod."

"I'm sorry," he said. "It's just one of those things."

"I understand," she said. But he knew she didn't.

Back in the interview room, the kid was still playing with the steel ring. Clank.

"Mountain Dew," the kid said, looking at the can.

"You don't like Mountain Dew?"

"Dew's okay." He popped open the can and took a sip.

"You were telling me about Jon Brande."

"Oh yeah. You know he sells dope, right?"

Rawls nodded. "We know about Jon's little business. One of these days we'll catch him with the goods."

"Well, he gave Mikey his stash the day of the locker search and Mikey lost it for him."

"Did you see the drugs?"

"No. I just saw Jon give Mikey a bag. Anyway, Mikey lost it and got punched in the mouth for his trouble, and Jon decided to make him pay for the dope. That's how I got involved."

8. MIKEY

I dressed extra-careful the next day: navy-blue suit, powder-blue shirt, black tie, my signature cuff links, and my two-tone (brown and black) wingtips. I guess I was thinking that maybe my split lip would attract less attention if I dazzled them all with fashion.

It didn't work. It got around school in a nanosecond what had happened. Instead of looking at my suit, everybody was staring at my mouth.

At least I didn't have to go around explaining it. Except to the new kid, Shayne, who was not yet hooked into the local information superhighway. He didn't say anything to me in class, but later on at lunch, as I was trying to eat a taco without ripping open the cut on my lip, he finally asked me what had happened to my face.

"I got in a fight." I thought he'd be impressed.

He wasn't. "It looks like you led with your mouth."

"I tend to do that," I said.

Shayne tore open the bag of chocolate chip cookies he'd bought for lunch. He stuffed one into his mouth and chewed, staring thoughtfully at my mouth.

"It's no big deal," I said.

He nodded.

I said, "Say, Shayne, I was wondering . . . since we're such good friends and all . . . do you have five hundred dollars I could borrow?"

Shayne took another bite, chewed, swallowed. "You mean because we've known each other a whole two days?"

I liked how he could be sort of sarcastic, only not in a mean way.

"What do you need the money for?" he asked.

I told him.

9. THE INTERVIEW ROOM

"I told Mikey I'd talk to Jon." The kid looked at Rawls with a flat expression. "I mean, even if Mikey hadn't shoved the bag in a trash can, he would have gotten caught with a bag full of whatever when he got hauled down to the office. So either way, Jon would have lost his stash. I thought maybe he'd listen to reason if it came from somebody other than Mikey. Mikey kind of pisses people off, you know?"

"I've met him," said Rawls. "The school locker thing."

"Are you the one who busted him for having Advil?"

Rawls shrugged. "He broke the rules."

"Stupid rule. You bust a kid for Advil while Jon Brande is selling weed."

Rawls agreed. The prohibition on Advil and other over-the-counter drugs was ridiculous, but it was his job to enforce the law—even minor infractions of a high school's "zero tolerance" rules.

"When we catch Jon with the goods, we'll bust him, too," he said.

Shayne clanked the ring back and forth a few times.

"I tried to talk to Jon about the Mikey thing," he said.

"How did that go?"

Clank.

"Not well."

10. MIKEY

Shayne said, "What's he going to do if you don't pay him?"

I pointed at my split lip. "What do you think?"

"If you had the money, would you pay him?"

"No way!" I said. But I was thinking I probably would. I really didn't want to get hit again.

"You say he's a dealer, so he must have some kind of business sense."

"Yeah. He knows if he threatens to kill you, he'll get his money."

"But if he kills you, you won't be able to pay him."

"But if I'm not going to pay him anyway, why not kill me?"

Shayne considered my logic—which was, I admit, not ironclad.

I said, "Jon is not what you'd call completely logical."

Shayne nodded. "But if we convince him that you just don't have the money . . . it won't hurt to talk to him."

"That's what you think." I made another effort to get my sore mouth around my taco as Shane looked around the lunchroom.

"That's him over there, right?" Shayne asked. "What are they doing?"

Jon was standing over by the snack machine, keeping

an eye out while Kyle Ness, one of his crew, reached up into the dispenser. I think Kyle's arms were triple-jointed. Trey Worthington stood next to them, using his massive body to block the view from the service counter.

"Kyle has arms like Mr. Fantastic," I said. "He's scoring free goodies."

"Who's the big guy?" Shayne asked.

"That's Trey Worthington, one of our football heroes." Kyle's arm came out with a bag of chips. He tossed it to Jon, then reached into the machine for more. "I think Jon supplies him with steroids. You do not want to mess with Trey." I hoped that would move Shayne off his idea that Jon could be reasoned with, but he just stood up and walked over to Jon and started talking. Jon got this grin on his face—the look he gets when he is about to have some nasty fun—and backed Shayne into the area between the vending machines. There was just enough room for the two of them, and it was out of sight of the food servers and lunchroom monitor.

A second later, Jon backed out and looked around the lunchroom with an even wider grin—the one he gets just after he's had some nasty fun.

Shayne was sitting on the floor between the machines holding his stomach and gasping for air. Your standard belly punch. It could have been a lot worse. Laughing, Jon and his minions took their free chips to their usual table in back.

I could have run over and helped him up—that would have been the stand-up thing to do—but I did not care to bring myself to Jon's attention just then. Or any other time. Instead, I ate the rest of my taco as Shayne slowly got to his feet and walked out of the lunchroom, a little hunched over.

II. THE INTERVIEW ROOM

"Did you report the incident?" Rawls asked.

The kid took a sip of his soda and looked Rawls in the eye "I'd only been at Wellstone a few days. I didn't want to start out being a snitch."

"Instead, you decided to start out by confronting the school drug dealer."

"Something like that. Only I didn't do anything. I mean, I let him hit me and didn't do anything."

"What did you want to do?"

"Break something. His nose. His arm."

"Lucky for Jon you restrained yourself," Rawls said with a smile.

The kid nodded, completely serious. "I didn't want to get kicked out for fighting."

I felt awful for Shayne after he got punched. But I felt even worse for myself, because now Jon would hold me personally responsible for sending Shayne as my ambassador. The fact that it wasn't my idea would not matter to Jon. He would probably give me a matching belly punch just for fun. I wondered how the taco I'd eaten would taste in reverse.

Fortunately, the 12:20 chime went off and I got out of the lunchroom and *escabullirsed* to Spanish class without having a Jon Brande moment.

I didn't see either Jon or Shayne the rest of the day, but I'd gotten Shayne's cell number that morning, so I texted him right after school, and he got back to me, and we met at the public library up on Thirty-third Street. It was the one place where I was absolutely sure we wouldn't run into Jon.

There is a big lobby in the front of the library where you can sit and talk and no one will bug you. I sat on one of the steel benches and played a game on my cell phone for half an hour before Shayne strolled in. He walked like he was on wheels, his shoulders perfectly level, his speed unvarying, his head moving slowly from side to side as he checked out the room. He saw me right away, and I waved him over.

"How's your gut?" I asked him.

"A little sore."

"You're lucky he didn't kick you in the nuts."

Shayne shrugged and sat down on the bench next to me.

"You shouldn't have tried to talk to him, you know."

"I figured it was worth a try. Next time I'll know."

"Know what?"

"What I'm dealing with."

"You don't deal with a guy like Jon. You avoid him."

"I know. But if you can't avoid him, then what?"

"You do what he wants."

"That's not an option," Shayne said. "Especially since you don't have the money."

"Maybe I can work out a payment plan. Five bucks a week for the rest of my life."

"You could report it."

"He'd just deny it. Then he'd beat the crap out of me."

"Not necessarily."

"You don't know Jon."

"I'm getting to know him better. You hungry?"

"Yeah, but I'm saving my money."

Shayne stood up. "Come on. I didn't get a chance to finish my lunch. There's a sub shop just up the street. I'll buy."

I never say no to free food. I figure if I eat enough, sooner or later I'll get a growth spurt.

On the way to the sub shop, Shayne said, "A guy like Jon Brande, it's important not to let him know you're afraid."

"I *am* afraid."

"But you don't show it."

"I don't?"

"You got that big mouth."

"Yeah, which is what got me beat up."

"It also protects you. Nobody, not even Jon Brande, wants to hear you say things they don't like. To them or anybody else."

I sat there without saying anything at all for about ten seconds, which had to be some kind of record for me.

"I don't think I can talk my way out of this," I said.

Shayne was staring into the distance. He said, "Tell me everything you know about Jon."

I didn't realize, until I tried to tell Shayne about Jon, how little I knew. He was a senior. He rode around on a black 1,300cc Suzuki crotch rocket; he sold drugs; he'd been dating my sister for the past few months. . . .

"What does your sister see in him?"

I ticked off five points on my fingers. "He's big; he looks good; he has money; he has a cool bike; he gives her free weed." I took the top off my sub so I could get my mouth around it. Smashed lips and meatball subs do not go good together.

"You'd think you being his girlfriend's brother and all he'd cut you some slack."

"Jon Brande cuts nobody slack."

Shayne thought for a moment. "Maybe we could talk to his parents. Where does he live?"

"I don't know."

"I bet your sister does."

After demolishing our subs we got on his bike, me without a helmet. Motorcycles scare me, but Shayne was a careful driver—no wheelies or anything—and his ancient BMW, for all its dents and duct tape, rode smooth as a limo. We arrived at my house without crashing or getting arrested. I got off the bike and pointed at the crotch rocket parked at the curb.

"That's Jon's bike," I said.

"Looks fast." He looked from the bike to the house, then at something in the bushes. "That your dog?"

It was. "Hey Barkie!" I yelled and clapped my hands. Barkie, my Jack Russell terrier, slunk out from his hiding spot and took a few tentative steps toward us, ears and tail down. I knelt on the grass and held my hands out. Barkie came closer, his tail wagging and drooping all at once.

"What's the matter with him?" Shayne asked.

"Jon Brande," I said.

13. MIKEY

When Marie first started going out with Jon I didn't really know him. I mean, I knew who he was, and that he sold dope, but I didn't know he was the sadistic spawn of Satan. I actually thought he was cool. But that all changed one Saturday afternoon. Marie had been seeing Jon for maybe a month. I had just come home from running errands for Mrs. Garcia. My parents weren't home. I found Jon and Marie out in the backyard gazebo smoking a joint.

This is how stupid and ignorant I was: I was impressed that Marie's boyfriend was a big, good-looking senior, with a big, good-looking bike. And I thought that their smoking a joint in the gazebo was sort of sophisticated. Not that I wanted to smoke myself—I'd heard that marijuana interferes with the production of growth hormones—but I appreciated the outlaw nature of the scene. I went out to the gazebo just to say hello. Barkie followed, wagging his stumpy tail so hard it was a blur.

Barkie was stupid and ignorant too, but he had an excuse: He was a dog.

Jon was showing something to Marie—it looked like an electric shaver or maybe a portable hair dryer.

"What's that?" I asked, all clueless and innocent.

"My new toy," Jon said, giving me that spectacular smile that I would come to hate.

Barkie, who was not getting enough attention, barked.

Marie said, "Mikey, why don't you and Barkie go play fetch or something?"

I ignored her. "What is it?" I asked Jon.

Barkie barked.

Jon said, looking at Barkie, "It's a bark stopper."

"A what?"

"Want to see how it works?"

Barkie must have sensed something about then; he backed out of the gazebo, barking furiously. Jon pointed the thing at Barkie and pressed a button. Something shot out of the end of it, two thin wires. Barkie collapsed and lay quivering on the lawn, his eyes wide with terror and pain.

I think I screamed. I could see two small darts stuck in Barkie's fur; I ran to him and yanked them out. Barkie's legs were jerking and his tongue was hanging out. I picked him up and hugged him to my chest.

"What did you do to him?" I shouted. Jon was doubled over laughing. Barkie whimpered and twitched in my arms. I was squeezing him too hard. I laid him down on the grass.

Jon said, "Don't worry, he'll be fine."

I must have been really mad, because I started toward Jon—all five-foot-nothing of me—with the intention of tearing him to pieces. Jon grabbed the end of the stun gun and pulled off this little plastic thing—later I learned it was the one-shot cartridge that shoots out the darts. He tossed the cartridge aside and pointed the gun at me. I stopped, bracing myself for a shock. He pressed the trigger. The end of the device snapped and crackled with blue lightning, but nothing shot out of it. I threw myself at him.

Jon jammed the stun gun against the side of my neck and my universe disintegrated.

What is it like to get umpteen thousand volts fired through your neck? First of all, it hurts. Like all of your pain receptors are rushing to one single nova-strength point of agony, and there is nothing you can do because your limbs are totally spazzing out and your thoughts are shattered to atoms and bouncing around your skull like there is no brain in between, and even though it only lasts a second or two it feels like forever.

Somewhere in the distance I could hear laughter. It was Jon, of course. I was on the ground, face in the grass. I heard my sister's voice, yelling. I turned my head and saw her hitting Jon on the shoulder with her fists. I had a moment of gratitude then—that she would care, even a little, that her boyfriend had electrocuted her brother and his dog.

Barkie struggled to his feet, shaking his head blearily. He looked at me, then at Jon, then walked off, his stumpy tail almost dragging, looking reproachfully back over his shoulder every few steps.

Jon said, "See? Your mutt's fine. No harm done."

He laughed.

"Barkie gets like that when Jon is around," I said to Shayne. "Ever since Jon tased him."

"He tased your *dog*?" That was the first time I saw Shayne look angry—his face hardened and his fists clenched so tightly his knuckles went bone-white.

"He didn't like the barking."

Shayne shook his head slowly. "You think he's inside?"

"I think he's around back in the gazebo with Marie. Probably getting high."

"Let's go talk to him," Shayne said. He started around the house. I followed. Barkie stayed behind.

I was wrong about them being in the gazebo. They were on the patio. Marie was sitting on the chaise doing Jon's math homework; Jon was standing over her. He had something in his hand. For a second I thought it was his stun gun, but it was his cell. He was texting someone. As we approached he looked up and gave us his smile. "Punching bag one and punching bag two," he said.

He wasn't looking at me, he was looking at Shayne—and Shayne was looking right back at him.

Jon said, "What are *you* looking at?"

"I'm trying to figure out what kind of jerk would use a stun gun on a little dog," Shayne said.

Jon's face darkened and the corners of his mouth drew back into a parody of a grin. "You better watch your mouth or I'll show *you* how it works."

"Go ahead." Shayne stood relaxed, arms loose at his sides, a faint curve to his lips that was almost—but not quite—a smile. I could feel something coming off him, a silent electric crackle, as if he was his own personal stun gun.

The two of them stared at each other. Jon's white grin stretched tight across his face, his every muscle rigid. I was pretty sure he didn't have the stun gun with him—it wasn't clipped to his belt, and it was too big to fit in his pockets.

Jon snorted and said, "Like I need it."

Shayne turned his hands out, silently inviting Jon to bring it on. Marie set her pencil down to watch, her dark lips parted in anticipation of boy violence. I don't know how long the staring contest went on. I was holding my breath, so it couldn't have been too long.

Finally, Jon looked away and said, "This is bull."

Marie giggled. I think it was just out of nervousness, but Jon didn't take it that way. His left hand shot out rattlesnake-fast and backhanded her across the face. Marie's head flew back, the chaise tipped, and she fell over.

Shayne didn't move. "Dogs and girls," he said, his eyes still on Jon.

"Next time," Jon said. He walked past Shayne—bumping his shoulder hard as he went by.

Shayne turned to watch him leave, then looked at Marie, who was holding a hand to her cheek.

"Are you okay?" he asked.

She nodded.

We heard the piercing snarl of Jon's bike revving, then the sound of him winding out through the gears as he took off.

Shayne walked up to Marie and touched her shoulder. "Are you sure?" he asked.

She lowered her hand to reveal four red stripes left by Jon's fingers. She looked down. "He's not always like that," she said. Which was exactly what Mom used to say about Dad.

I said, "Shayne, this is my sister, Marie."

"Nice to meet you, Marie," Shayne said.

"Shayne's new," I said.

Marie wiped her eyes with the back of her hand, looked up at Shayne, and smiled. She had a nice smile, but she didn't use it often. Shayne took her hand and helped her up.

"Thank you." She pushed her hair away from her face and gave him that up-and-down look that girls usually do only when the guy isn't looking. "You're cute," she said.

For most of my life my sister has been a mystery to me. For one thing, she used to be incredibly smart. She had no problem with the schoolwork—learning came easy to her. But back in the eighth grade, around the same time Dad quit drinking—also about the same time her boobs got big—it was as if she'd taken a stupid pill. She didn't study, she spent hours on her hair and makeup, the only reading she did was magazines, and she went through one idiot boyfriend after another, usually the biggest loser she could land. Jon Brande was her Holy Grail, and she had finally reeled him in a few months back.

One theory I had was that she wanted whichever guy was most like Dad back when he'd been drinking. Only now, seeing the way she was looking at Shayne, I had to revise that theory. It wasn't about her wanting guys who were like Dad—Shayne was nothing like him at all—so it had to be something else, and I thought I knew what it was.

Marie liked Shayne because of what we could all see, but nobody was saying out loud: Jon was afraid of him.

Mom was in the kitchen chopping onions when the three of us went inside. I introduced her to Shayne.

He said, "Nice to meet you, ma'am."

I could tell she liked being called ma'am because she immediately offered Shayne a soda.

"No thank you," he said, politely.

Mom liked Shayne so much she invited him to stay for dinner. In our house we almost always ate one of two things: beans and rice, or pasta. It's not as boring as it sounds—Mom knew a million variations of each. That night it was black beans with chunks of bacon, her famous "dirty rice," and a huge bowl of fresh strawberries for dessert. Who could say no to that?

Marie flirted like crazy all though dinner, and to my horror, Shayne ate it up right along with his beans and rice. It was embarrassing. My mom saw it too, and she got this little smile on her face. I think she was happy to see Marie interested in someone other than Jon. Even Barkie took to Shayne right away, sitting attentively beside him all through dinner.

We were almost done eating when Dad got home from work. Shayne stood up and shook his hand and called him sir, like he was in the army.

My father, as I've mentioned, is a recovering alcoholic. It's been three years since he's had a drink. Ever since then, he's been out to prove to everybody just how perfect he can be. Especially to my sister. He treats her like a princess, and the nicer he is to her, the more bratty she gets. But, with Shayne there, Marie was on her best behavior.

Dad asked Shayne a lot of questions. Shayne told him that he was living with his aunt, that he'd grown up in Arkansas, and that his parents were doctors spending the year in Uganda giving people vaccinations and stuff. I almost said something, because that was a completely different story than he'd told me.

"What organization are they with?" Dad asked.

Shayne didn't miss a beat. "Doctors Without Borders," he said.

My dad ate a forkful of rice, chewed for a few seconds, swallowed, then said, "That's a fine organization. You should be proud."

"I *am* proud," said Shayne, as Marie gave him her patented look of adoration.

Dad looked from me to Shayne, then back at me with a sad expression. He didn't say anything, but I knew what he was thinking as he looked at me: *Why can't you be more like* him?

What I said before about Shayne being nothing like my dad? Not quite true. They both put a ridiculous amount of effort into being perfect—like the way Shayne was so polite and restrained, as if holding himself in, and the way Dad always thought for a second or two before speaking, as if they both had a belly full of TNT, and any sudden movement might cause them to explode.

Later, Shayne and I were in the backyard kicking a soccer ball, and I asked him how come he told so many different stories about his parents.

"They're really not very interesting," Shayne said. "My dad's a computer programmer in Atlanta, and my mom's in New York working for some bank."

"So how come you're living with your aunt?"

He juggled the soccer ball, keeping it in the air with one foot, then kicked it straight up. I tried to header it back to him but hit it wrong and the ball bounced over the fence into Mrs. Garcia's garden.

"Oops." I grabbed the top of the wooden fence and pulled myself up to see where the ball had gone. "Uh-oh." One of Mrs. Garcia's peonies was completely squashed.

"I'll get it," Shayne said.

"Watch out for—"

He was up and over the fence in an instant.

"—the dog!"

Shayne had reached the ball when Cujo came roaring out of the house through the dog door and charged at him, barking as loud and fast as ten dogs. Shayne grabbed the ball and took off, but I could see he wouldn't make it over the fence in time. Cujo latched on to his leg just as he reached the fence. Shayne threw the ball over the fence and tried to shake the dog off, but Cujo, teeth locked on his pant leg, was going nowhere.

Mrs. Garcia banged open the back door and screeched: "Cujo! Down, girl!"

The six-pound Chihuahua let go, gave Shayne a series of admonishing barks and growls, then trotted back to the house, snorting and shaking its head indignantly. Shayne climbed over the fence with an embarrassed grin on his face.

"*Cujo?*" he said.

I was laughing too hard to reply.

The next day I wore my red blazer with a pair of dark maroon pants. I looked a little like an usher or a bell boy, only much classier.

Shayne showed up in American Lit the same as always—calm, quiet, watchful, and dressed in black. We were taking turns reading out loud from an Edgar Allan Poe story so I didn't get a chance to talk to him. He didn't show up at lunch. I was sitting alone with my bean burrito and milk when I felt a presence looming over me. I knew without looking that it was Jon Brande.

"Little Mikey," he said in a fake-friendly voice.

I tipped my head back to see Jon's upside-down face staring at me.

"You got my money?"

"You mean the money I don't owe you?" I said.

"I mean the money for the stuff you threw in the garbage." He sat down next to me, grabbed a handful of chips from my plate, and ate one, crunching it with his mouth open and grinning at the same time.

I said, "If I hadn't, they would have found it when they searched me."

"Not my problem." Crunch. "But I don't want you to think I'm unreasonable." He grabbed some more chips. "Here's the deal. You're going to like this. Pay me a hundred on Wednesday, then a hundred every week. Like an E-Z payment plan." Crunch.

I should have said, *Buzz off, Brande. I don't owe you a dime.*

But I enjoy being alive, with all four limbs working, so I took a bite of my burrito to keep myself from saying anything. Jon stood up, patted me on the head, and started toward his table. Then he stopped, as if he'd just thought of something, and turned back to me.

"That friend of yours . . . what's his name?"

It wasn't hard to figure out who he was talking about. "Shayne?" I said.

"Yeah, him. What's his deal?"

"I have no idea." It was true.

Jon took a couple of seconds to decide whether or not I was lying, then he nodded. "That piece-a-crap bike I saw in front of your house yesterday—that his?"

"It's a BMW," I said.

"I *know* it's a BMW. I asked you if it was *his.*"

"Yeah, it's his." Just then I saw Shayne come into the lunchroom.

Jon followed my glance, saw Shayne, smiled that creepy smile he does so well, and sauntered back to his table to join Kyle and Trey.

Shayne sat down in the same chair Jon had been in.

I said, "Jon's decided to put me on his 'E-Z payment plan.'"

Shayne grabbed one of my chips. I might as well have had a sign: FREE CHIPS.

"A hundred a week," I said.

Shayne didn't say anything.

"But you better watch out," I said. "He was asking about your bike."

"What about it?"

"If it was yours."

Shayne looked back at Jon's table. Jon was talking to Trey Worthington, who was staring fixedly at Shayne.

"He's going to do something," I said.

Shayne sighed wearily. "I know."

16. MIKEY

Trey Worthington would never have made it past the ninth grade if it wasn't for the fact that he was enormous. Size matters. It really does. Mr. Benno, the football coach, latched on to Trey around the time he hit two hundred pounds. Benno had used his tutoring abilities and his influence with the other teachers to keep Trey in school and on the football team for four brutal, head-bashing seasons. But now Trey was a senior, football season was over, and Mr. Benno's moderating presence no longer mattered—he had been replaced by Jon Brande as Trey's puppet master.

Just a few weeks ago, Jon had said, "Hey, Trey, why don't you head-butt that locker and see how big a dent you can make?"

Trey had head-butted Jason Aiken's locker and dented it so bad the door had to be replaced. Trey was fine, or at least no worse than before.

It made perfect sense that Jon would sic Trey on Shayne.

After school I caught up with Shayne and walked out with him, hoping for a ride home. I figured if we left right away, there would be less chance of a Jon encounter.

We weren't fast enough. Jon, Trey, and Kyle were waiting by the line of motorcycles in the student lot. All three
of them rode motorcycles—their own little biker gang.
Jon was sitting astride his enormous crotch rocket talking
with Marie. Kyle, leaning against his slightly smaller version of Jon's Suzuki, was cleaning his fingernails with the
triangular blade of a utility knife. Trey stood on the other
side of Shayne's BMW, watching us walk toward him. He
waited until we were about twenty feet away, then put his
size fourteen shoe against the BMW and shoved. The bike
crashed to the ground.

"Oops," he said.

Shayne, looking down at his fallen bike, shook his
head slowly.

"Your bike fell down," said Trey. Jon and Kyle laughed.
Marie took a few steps back, watching with that pseudo-
bored look girls get when boys are about to do something
incredibly stupid but potentially exciting.

Shayne raised his eyes to look first at Jon, then at Trey.
I searched the parking lot for some sort of adult intervention, but there were no teachers in sight.

Shayne said, "You don't have to do this."

Trey grinned and shrugged his colossal shoulders.
Shayne bent over and grabbed the handlebars of his bike
and lifted it back onto its stand. The bike must have outweighed him by a couple hundred pounds; Shayne made
it look easy. The rearview mirror hung, shattered and
twisted, from the fall.

"Your mirror's broke," Trey said. They were standing
on opposite sides of the bike.

Shayne looked over at Jon and said, "I'll send *you* a bill."

Jon laughed and looked at Trey. Trey raised his foot and tried to topple the bike again. Shayne's hand shot out, cupped the back of his ankle, and heaved. Trey, off balance, hopped back on one leg, then fell.

Jon, laughing, said, "Whoa! Dude!"

Trey jumped to his feet and went after Shayne. That was the part where any normal person would have taken off running, but Shayne just backed away a few steps and stood with his arms loose at his sides, hands open, feet spread.

"Don't," he said.

Trey wasn't listening. He aimed a skull-crushing blow at Shayne's head.

Impossibly, he missed. Shayne drew his head back at the exact right instant, almost casually, as if he knew what was going to happen a tenth of a second before it did. Trey's fist missed him by inches.

"Don't," Shayne said again.

Trey swung again. Shayne ducked under the punch and thrust his elbow up to strike Trey in the triceps. Trey let out a grunt of pain and backed off, grabbing the back of his arm.

"Stop," Shayne said.

Trey, cursing and scowling at Shayne, shook out his arm and flexed it a few times, waiting for the feeling to return.

"It'll be fine," said Shayne.

Trey threw himself at Shayne, this time with both arms

outstretched. Instead of moving back, Shayne stepped into the embrace. There was this frozen moment when I imagined they were about to hug each other, but Shayne went in low—Trey's arms grabbed nothing, his feet came off the ground, and he was in the air, head pointed straight down, four feet above the asphalt parking lot, as his feet pedaled sky. Time slowed, then sped up. Trey's legs went up and over and he landed flat on his back. I could feel the earth shake when he hit.

Even before Trey hit the ground, Shayne had stepped away and turned so that he was facing an astonished-looking Jon and Kyle. Trey, flat on his back, stared pop-eyed at the sky, making *heek-heek* sounds, followed by a shuddering, wheezy gasp.

Shayne's attention was fixed on Jon and Kyle. Kyle's thumb worked the slide on his utility knife, the razor-sharp blade snicking in and out like a cat's claw.

Trey coughed and climbed to his hands and knees. He gave Shayne a look that contained equal measures of anger, bewilderment, and respect.

Shayne offered him a hand up. Trey slapped it away and lurched to his feet.

Shayne stepped back, once again assuming that loose, ready stance. Trey clenched and unclenched his fists.

Jon forced out a laugh. "Better chill, Trey. Five-O."

I looked over to see Mr. Benno jogging toward us from the school entrance. Kyle retracted the blade of his knife, slipped it into his pocket, and straddled his motorcycle. Jon started his bike and slapped his thigh, as if calling a dog.

"Let's go, shorty," he said to Marie.

Marie gave Shayne a weak smile, then climbed onto the back of Jon's bike. Jon pointed his finger at me and said, "Wednesday, Mikey." They took off, followed by Kyle.

Trey stayed where he was, glaring at Shayne as if he was disappointed at not getting another shot at him, but it seemed to me that the main thing he was feeling was relief.

Seconds later, Mr. Benno arrived, all out of breath and trying not to show it. "Is there a problem here?" he asked.

"No problem," Shayne said. "Trey here accidentally knocked my bike over. No harm done."

Mr. Benno looked at the broken mirror. He seemed about to argue, then gave his head a little shake, deciding it would be a lot easier to let it go.

"Perhaps you should apologize," he said to Trey.

Trey scowled, but apparently Mr. Benno, his former coach, still had some influence over him. "Sorry," he muttered.

"All right, then!" said Mr. Benno, clapping both Trey and Shayne on their backs as if he'd just brokered peace in the Middle East. "Let's not have any more nonsense." He walked off.

Shayne said to Trey, "So are we cool?"

Trey turned his back and walked over to his bike. *So much for peace in the Middle East,* I thought. Trey started to get on his bike, then hesitated and said something I couldn't hear.

Shayne said, "What?"

Trey said, "How did you know to do that?" He moved

his hand in a circle, which I understood to represent his 280-pound body flying through the air. "That thing you did."

I'd been wondering the same thing.

Shayne said, "My dad showed me."

Trey shook his head. "That was wild," he said, then got on his bike and rode off.

Later, as Shayne was giving me a lift home, I said, "Trey used to be a nice guy."

"I never said he wasn't a nice guy," said Shayne.

"He just tried to beat you up."

"That wasn't Trey. It was Jon."

He was right, of course. But how many guys would see it that way?

17. THE INTERVIEW ROOM

George Rawls liked to think that he understood teenagers. After all, he had once been one. And before he'd become a cop he had spent a year, part of a year, teaching high school. And he had two teenage nephews—his sister's kids. They weren't all that complicated. One part genius, one part idiot, and three parts peer pressure. Throw in a handful of rampant sexual energy and a dash of geeky awkwardness and you had it: Teen Boy.

This kid, though . . . this kid he didn't get at all.

For one thing, there was a *calmness* there, even though the kid was clearly in pain—whatever he had done, he was hurting from it. But when he spoke it was in this matter-of-fact voice, as if he was reading from a script only he could see. And he was taking his time.

Rawls said, "So you had a fight with this kid Trey. But he was okay?"

"He was fine. It was just a scuffle, really."

Rawls sat back and scratched his head. He tried not to do that because someone had once told him that scratching your head would cause baldness. More hair loss he did not need. But it helped him think. Maybe it increased blood flow to the brain. He scratched some more, then said, "Listen, kid, I know you got this big long story for me, and not that I don't appreciate it, but I don't see how this incident with Trey is important."

"It's important because of what happened later."

Rawls sighed and made a reeling motion with his hand: on with the show. The kid took another sip of soda, then continued.

"I knew Jon wasn't going to let it go, so after the thing with Trey I thought I'd go see Jon's dad. It turned out to be sort of a bad idea."

"How so?" Rawls asked.

"Well, for one thing, his dad was kind of a jerk."

Rawls waited.

"I went over to his house that same afternoon. I figured Jon wouldn't be home. I rang the doorbell. Finally, a guy answered who looked like Jon only way older and fifty pounds heavier. He was wearing boxers and a T-shirt. I think I woke him up from a nap.

"He said, 'Who the hell are you?'

"I told him my name and asked him if he was Jon's dad. He wanted to know why I cared, so I told him."

"Told him what?"

"That Jon was threatening other students."

"Did you tell him Jon was selling drugs?"

"I might have mentioned it."

"What did he say?"

"He just stared at me for a while—you know that look a guy gets when he's trying to decide whether to hit you? Then he said if I ever came around there again he'd kick my ass. Then he slammed the door.

PETE HAUTMAN

"So I figured that explained a lot about Jon. You know, how he got to be the way he was. Anyway, I was just leaving when Jon pulled into the driveway on his bike. He just sat there and stared at me."

"What did you do?"

"I got on my bike and rode off."

"That's it?"

"I wouldn't say that. Something happened after I left. But I didn't find out about it until the next day."

18. MIKEY

Money. I do have an income, sort of. Mrs. Garcia, three doors down, who refuses to leave her house due to her pathological fear of squirrels, pays me to run errands for her. Like picking up things from the grocery or her prescriptions from Banner Drug. She's good for twenty or thirty dollars a week, depending on how many errands I run. Sometimes she forgets to pay me, but she always tells me how nice I look. She is one of the few people who truly appreciates the care I take with my appearance. In fact, that's where most of my money goes. Clothes. Not that I pay full retail. I buy my clothes at thrift stores. There's a good one over near the synagogue where there are always new suits in my size coming in—all those thirteen-year-old Jewish kids wear them once for their bar mitzvah then grow out of them. Most of the suits are pretty dark-colored and boring—I think a bar mitzvah must be something like a happy funeral—but they fit me fine because of my diminutive stature. But they are not free, and dry cleaning costs money too. And even if I quit buying new clothes and gave every dime I earned to Jon Brande, it would take me months to come up with five hundred dollars.

Mrs. Garcia's Saturday morning grocery order was usually too heavy to carry, so I borrowed Mom's three-wheel gardening cart and walked it over to Jerry's Shop-n-Save. I rolled the cart right into the store. They let me do that because I am a regular.

There were about twenty items on the list, including English muffins, baking potatoes, liverwurst, graham crackers, ginger snaps, and a case of chocolate Ensure. You know what Ensure is? I drank one once. It's like a thick, slimy version of chocolate milk. Old people chug them like Red Bulls.

I noticed that almost everything on her list was brown, so I added a bunch of bright yellow bananas, a head of lettuce, and two red apples to the cart. Mrs. Garcia likes me to be creative. I threw in a can of root beer and a Slim Jim for myself. Have you ever read the ingredients list on a Slim Jim? Love those "mechanically separated chicken parts."

Mrs. Garcia must have just got her Social Security check; she paid me with a crisp twenty dollar bill. That increased my total cash supply to $27.92. No way would I come up with $100.00 by Wednesday. I was thinking about that as I rolled the cart back into the garage, and I was still thinking about it when I went into the house, but then I stopped thinking when I saw Shayne sitting at the kitchen counter with Marie.

Marie saw me come in and made a face.

I made a face back at her. Shayne looked at the two of us in that way he had: measuring, evaluating, computing.

"What's up?" I said.

"Shayne was telling me about when he grew up," Marie said.

"You grew up?" I said. Maybe I was being a little bit sarcastic, but I really meant it, in a way. I guess I had this feeling about Shayne even then, that he hadn't ever been a little kid, that he had always been exactly the same.

Also—this is embarrassing—I think I was a little bit jealous. Like Marie was trying to steal him from me.

"You didn't tell me he was originally from Australia," Marie said.

Australia? I looked at Shayne and thought I detected a faintly self-conscious smile on his lips. "Let me guess. You were raised by kangaroos in the outback?"

"Aborigines," Shayne said with a straight face.

"Of course."

Marie wasn't getting that it was a joke. She was all in lust. Seeing Shayne toss Trey Worthington over his shoulder like a sack of potatoes must have given her a hormonal overdose. Even if she wasn't my sister, I think I'd have found it somewhat repellent.

"I thought you grew up in Arkansas," I said. "Or Idaho."

"There too," he said without hesitating.

"And are your parents doctors, or spies, or aboriginies?"

"All three."

Marie said to him, "You're funny." It came out like, *You're hot.*

"I am a maze of contradictions," Shayne said, still with that hint of a smile.

"Me too," Marie said. "I contradict myself amazingly often."

"I think you're both insane," I said.

"You shouldn't say that," Shayne said, suddenly serious. "Insanity is no joke."

"What should I say then? You're in la-la land? You're nut jobs? Crunk monkeys?"

Shane gave me about two seconds of nothing, then asked, "What's a crunk monkey?"

"I have no crunking idea."

Shayne's mouth softened, then formed a smile, and then he was laughing. Marie started laughing too. I, who was no crunk monkey, turned my back and went to my room.

Shayne had dinner with the four of us again that night. Marie was being talkative for a change, and at one point she mentioned a book she had read.

"Since when do you read books?" I said. I hadn't seen her read a book since the seventh grade.

"Now Michael . . ." Mom started her usual dinner table intervention, but Marie was on a roll.

"Since forever," she said. "What do you think I do in my room all the time? Work on my hair?"

"Actually, yeah."

"I read all the Gossip Girls. I read *Pride and Prejudice*. I read that vampire book . . ."

"*Dracula?*" Dad asked.

"No. The one where the vampire is a good guy, and this other guy turns into a wolf."

"Did you read the actual books, or the comic book versions?" I asked.

Marie gave me a scathing return look. "Mikey, you're a moron." She batted her eyes at Shayne. "Is *moron* okay? Or is it too close to *insane*?"

"Now Marie . . ." Mom began, then trailed off as she saw Shayne open his mouth.

"*Moron*'s okay, but Mikey's not a moron," Shayne said.

"Right—he just says moronic things," Marie said.

"Nobody here is a moron," Mom said. She offered Shayne the bread basket for the third time. I think she wanted to adopt him.

I said, "Better to say stupid stuff than to do it."

"Saying is doing," Marie said. "When you *say* something you are *doing* something. You are *saying*."

"You mean if I say, 'I'm brilliant,' it's the same as *being* brilliant?"

"No. What you're *doing* is *saying*."

"Yeah, well I say you're a crunk monkey."

Dad had clamped his jaw shut and was looking off into the distance. I wondered what would have come out of his mouth if he hadn't been working so hard to keep it in.

Shayne must have noticed it too. He said, "Mr. Martin, how does it feel to live in a house filled with philosophers?"

"Philosophers?" He gave Shayne an uncomprehending look.

Shayne said, "Yeah, like the nature of reality: If you say something, does that make it real? Like when Mikey says, 'crunk monkey,' does that mean crunk monkeys actually exist?"

Dad looked at Shayne with an odd, brow-crinkling expression—maybe trying to figure out if he was being teased.

Shayne said, "It's exactly like philosophy, only without all the—you know—logic and stuff. And with crunk monkeys."

Dad said, "What *is* a 'crunk monkey?'"

"Apparently, *I* am a crunk monkey," said Marie, giving me her squinchy face.

Dad laughed; it was like a balloon popping. All the tension went out of the room, tension I hadn't even known was there.

Dad loosened up and asked Shayne who he favored in the next presidential election.

"Dad, he doesn't care about politics," I said. "He can't even vote!"

"Just because you're too young to vote doesn't mean you shouldn't know who you would vote for if you could vote," Dad said. Like crunk monkey logic, that made sense only if you didn't think about it too hard.

Shayne said, "Who will *you* be voting for, sir?"

Dad told him, then spent an eternity explaining why. Shayne listened attentively, nodding in all the right places. By the time he finished, Dad had convinced himself that everyone at the table agreed with everything he had said. Of course, nobody disagreed because nobody wanted to keep talking about it.

I don't want to give the impression that my dad is as boring as a crunk monkey. But he can be tedious when it comes to certain subjects. Politics, for example. Or submersible pumps. Do *not* get him started on submersible pumps. He engineers pumps for his job, and engineers are the most boring people on the planet when they talk about their work. He can go on about pumps for hours.

Once we were done discussing politics, Marie tried to move the conversation on to recent movies. Bad idea. The last movie my parents went to was *Schindler's List*, before I was born. But that didn't stop Dad from talking about it all the way through dessert. Shayne's attentive nodding became robotic, and Marie was rolling her eyes so hard I could almost hear them squeak. Finally, I interrupted him and said Shayne and I were hoping to shoot some baskets before it got dark.

Once Shayne and I got outside I said, "Sorry about my dad."

"Why?" Shayne asked.

"He can go on a bit."

"I like your dad," he said. "He's intense."

"I like him too, but he's my *dad*." I grabbed the basketball and made a jump shot from the side. Swish.

"HORSE," I said, and passed the ball to Shayne.

My dad, who is six feet two inches tall, put up the basketball net when I was in kindergarten. It took me until the second grade to make my first basket. From that moment on, I dreamed of becoming the next Shaquille O'Neal. I got pretty good for a guy my size—but I'm still waiting for that growth spurt.

Shayne duplicated my shot. I dribbled the ball halfway down the driveway and sank an underhanded lob.

"You're lucky," Shayne said.

"Pure skill," I said.

"I mean, you're lucky to have such a great dad."

"Oh." I didn't know what to say to that. Shayne's dad was in Afghanistan or wherever, and here I was complaining about my father's social skills.

He missed the shot.

"That's an *H* for you," I said. "And you're right. My dad's okay."

"I like your sister, too." Shayne laughed at the expression on my face. "Don't worry, I'm not going to ask her out or anything."

Immediately, I did a mental flip-flop—I didn't like that Marie was hot for him, but at the same time, it bugged me that he wouldn't want to go out with her.

"Why not?" I said.

"I just don't want to get tangled up."

"You got tangled up with Jon Brande," I pointed out, going in for an easy lay-up.

Shayne said, "I went over to his house yesterday."

I missed the shot. "Please tell me you're kidding."

"I talked to his dad. Well, sort of talked to him." Shayne retrieved the ball and made a two-handed overhead shot from six feet behind the free throw line. "He told me to get lost."

"I hope Jon doesn't find out," I said.

Shayne shrugged.

We were tied at *H-O-R* when my dad came outside and started fiddling with the birdbath fountain in the side yard. The fountain had stopped working a few days before. He looked up, caught Shayne's eye, and waved him over.

"Oh no," I said.

Naturally, the fountain was powered by a submersible pump. Five minutes later, Shayne and my dad were in the garage disassembling the pump, and I was shooting free throws all by myself.

Later that night I was in my room working on my Trig homework when I looked up to see Marie standing in my doorway, pajamas on, arms crossed, leaning against the jamb.

"What's the deal with Shayne?" she asked.

"What do you mean?" I asked.

"You know. Does he have a girlfriend?"

"Not as far as I know. I've only known him a few days."

"Jon doesn't like him much," she said.

"Jon doesn't like anybody."

"He likes me. Sort of."

I didn't say anything to that. She looked around my room as if seeing it for the first time. "You're very neat," she said.

"I like to know where things are."

She half-smiled. "You were always that way. Putting your own clothes away when you weren't even in kindergarten. This four-year-old neat freak."

I didn't take offense at that. It was true.

She said, "He should watch out. Shayne, I mean. He shouldn't make Jon mad."

"It wasn't his fault. Shayne just tried to talk to Jon about the five hundred I supposedly owe him, which I don't. Anyways, I don't have it."

"Doesn't Mrs. Garcia pay you every week?"

"Not *that* much."

Marie thought for a moment, then sighed. "I guess I could try to talk to him again."

"*Again?*"

"I tried to talk to him once. I didn't want to see you get tased again. I thought maybe if you paid him a little bit every week, it would work out."

"That was *your* idea?"

"It was the best I could do."

"Oh. Well, thanks, I guess."

"Maybe if I tell him you really don't have the money, he'll forget about it."

"How come you're being nice to me all of a sudden?"

"I shouldn't be nice to my baby brother?"

"I'm not used to it, that's for sure."

"Shayne's nice," she said. "He listens when I talk."

"So you've decided to be nice too?" Even as I said it, it hit me: That was exactly right. Marie had a fetish for the top dog in the pound, as her list of current and former boyfriends proved, but she also had this personality defect—okay, *quirk*—that made her act like whatever guy she was fixated on. With Jon, it was all about being totally self-centered and not caring about anybody else. But now, for the first time, my sister had found herself panting after a dog who was actually a nice guy.

20. MIKEY

I had homework for this class called Cultural Studies where I had to analyze some aspect of American culture as compared to some other culture. I chose fashion for my cultural aspect and Haitian for my other culture. Then I made a list of every article of clothing I owned, and then I went over to Pépé and Mémé's apartment to complete my research.

Pépé and Mémé are my grandparents. Those aren't really their names but that's what they like me to call them. I think it means "grandpa" and "grandma" in Haitian.

Pépé answered the door and gave me a bony hug.

Mémé came running out from the kitchen and gave me a squishy hug, then she rushed back into the kitchen, her long red hair flying, and immediately started cooking. It was only a matter of seconds before I heard a handful of onions hit the hot lard. She thinks if I eat more rice and beans and pork fat, I'll get taller. It hasn't worked yet, but I'm willing to keep trying.

I told Pépé about my school project and asked him what clothes he had when he was my age. He crinkled his eyes at me and got out the checkerboard.

Pépé loves his checkers. I figured I'd have to let him kick my butt at least three games in a row to get the information I needed. We set up the board and six moves later I was down two men. I don't know how he does it.

"I was a very sharp dresser, your age," Pépé said. "Like you." Pépé has a strong accent. He didn't speak much English until he was an adult so it came more like, *I beddy shop dressou, you aich. Lie gyoo.* But don't worry—I will translate.

"Only we did not have suits and ties like you wear sometimes. Too hot and no money."

I should mention that I was not wearing a suit at that time. On weekends I prefer more casual outfits. That day I wore khakis, loafers, and a maroon crew neck sweater— what Marie calls my 1980s preppie look. Not that she was even alive back then. I don't know where she gets that stuff.

"Your age, I had only four shirts, but I always kept them very clean. One for church, white. One for school. One paisley. Do you know paisley?"

I knew paisley, a strange, colorful, swirly pattern—very ugly, but I didn't say that.

"That was for special occasions." He moved one of his checkers forward, offering me a jump. I went for it, but of course it was a trap. He came back at me with a triple jump.

"King me," he said with a yellow grin.

I king'd him.

"And one T-shirt the color of the Haitian flag—red, white, blue, and a little green. I wore that one a lot."

"What about pants?"

"Polyester. Everything was polyester. Bell bottom."

I was disappointed. I'd been hoping he'd worn grass shirts or some sort of voodoo robes, which would have made my report more interesting. I tried to imagine Pépé at sixteen, with his purple-black skin, wearing a paisley shirt and polyester bellbottoms. He would be smiling—Pépé always smiled—and thinking about . . . what? Getting out of Haiti? No, he was probably thinking about girls. Pépé had an eye for pretty young girls, though he always said he'd never met one as pretty as Mémé.

"What about other kids?"

"Mostly the same, only I always looked very sharp. Your grandmama could not resist me."

"I could have resisted easy," Mémé shouted from the kitchen. "Only I saw how I maybe could fix you!"

Pépé laughed. "You fix me good!" he said. As he jumped his way to an easy checkers victory, he told me more about his teenage years: fishing on the piers, how many girlfriends he'd had, and how a lot of his classmates got involved with the teenage gangs in Port-au-Prince.

"But not me, no. I have no truck with gangs. I go to work instead." He flexed his large long-fingered hands. "I make things for to sell. That is how I meet your grandmama."

"He was selling voodoo dolls for the tourists," Mémé yelled from the kitchen. "I had to kick him off the sidewalk."

Pépé chuckled. "Your grandmama has ears like a cat. But it is true. I was selling in front of her mama's shop. But I charm her."

"He was very charming," Mémé said.

As we set up the board for another game, he asked me how school was going. Pépé was always curious about high school. He had only an eighth-grade education, so to him the higher grades were like a mythical world in which the secrets of the universe were being taught. My world was as mysterious to him as his Haitian childhood was to me.

I found myself telling him about how a lot of kids were using drugs. He asked me how they got them. I told him about Jon Brande. I don't know why, but I had always found it easy to tell Pépé things I would never tell my parents. He was a good listener, and he never tut-tutted me or made me feel stupid.

"This boy, he sounds like a *djab*," he said.

"What's that?"

"A spirit person. Powerful and most dangerous. You avoid him?"

"I try. Only he thinks I owe him money, so . . ."

Pépé became serious. "You borrow money from this *djab*?"

"No!"

"François, don't you be filling that boy's head up with that nonsense!" Mémé shouted from the kitchen.

Pépé rolled his eyes and winked at me. He moved a checker forward and lowered his voice. "You need money?"

I shook my head. I knew Pépé and Mémé had hardly enough money to get by. Pépé worked as a janitor for an insurance company downtown, and Mémé had a part-time job teaching French at a charter school. I wasn't about to give their rent money to Jon Brande.

For a few minutes we played checkers without talking. I saw an opportunity and made what I thought was a sneaky move, but Pépé said, "You do not want to do that."

"Why?"

"Look at the board."

I looked at the board, and after a few seconds I saw the trap he had laid for me. I took my move back.

"You must always think three moves ahead," he said.

"Three's a lot."

"Not so much if you use your *tête*."

I used my *tête*—that means "head"—and came up with another move.

"Better," said Pépé. "What you going to do about this *djab*?"

"I don't know. I have a friend, he says to not pay. Now Jon's mad at him, too." I told him about Shayne and about the fight with Trey. Pépé listened. When I'd finished talking, he reached out a long index finger and slid a checker forward.

"Now you got two *djabs*," he said.

"Trey's a *djab* too?"

"No. The boy who fights for you."

"Shayne's not a *djab*, he's a good guy," I said.

"*Djabs* are not good or bad. Maybe they cancel each other out."

Mémé came out with two glasses of lemonade and plunked them down on the table. "Don't listen to this crazy old man," she said. "You have a problem with a boy at school, you go to your teachers. Or the police." She stomped back to the kitchen.

Pépé leaned over the checkerboard and whispered, "She does not understand *djabs*."

Monday morning, six forty-five, I was in my underwear trying to decide between my navy-blue double-breasted and my charcoal-gray three-piece when I heard a motor-cycle engine, then a *bleet-bleet* from the driveway. I looked out my bedroom window to see Jon Brande sitting on his bike. Something was wrong with his face. I put on my glasses for a better look. Jon had a black eye. Two seconds later, Marie flew out of the house and hopped on the back of the bike and they took off.

I decided on the double-breasted, got dressed, and went downstairs. My mom was holding the curtain aside and staring out the window at the empty driveway.

"Honking like that." Mom shook her head. "That boy's mother must not have taught him any manners."

"I don't think he has a mom," I said.

"Well, it certainly shows."

"Marie says his mom took off when he was five."

"That's awful!"

"Maybe that's why he's such a jerk. Do we have any frosted flakes?"

"Why don't you have some *un*frosted flakes for a change?"

"They don't have frosting."

She let the curtain fall back into place and turned to me. Her eyes did that up-and-down thing. "*You* look nice," she said.

Shayne was in a quiet mood that morning, even for Shayne. I watched him slumped at his desk in American Lit, staring at a point in space a few feet in front of his eyes. I kept thinking about what Pépé had suggested—that Shayne was a *djab.* I knew Pépé had been kidding me. But then again, with Pépé, I never knew for sure.

After class I walked with Shayne to the east wing, where we both had our next classes. I talked the whole way—I don't remember about what. Shayne hardly said a word.

I hadn't seen Jon or Marie all morning. At lunch, Kyle and Trey were sitting at their usual table, but no Jon. Shayne showed up a few minutes late, bought a slice of pizza, and joined me.

"Hey," I said.

He peeled off a piece of pepperoni and ate it. I asked him if anything was wrong. He shook his head. Kyle and Trey were staring at us, their eyes like laser sights.

"I shouldn't have got in that fight with Trey," Shayne said.

"It didn't look to me like you had a choice."

He shook his head. "There's always a choice. If you think far enough ahead."

I thought of Pépé's checkers advice.

"I saw Jon this morning," I said. "He picked up Marie."

Shayne nodded.

"He had a black eye."

Shayne smiled.

"Do you know how he got it?" I asked.

"It wasn't from me."

Jon never showed up at school that day. Neither did Marie. She didn't come home for dinner, either. Mom was frantic, calling Marie's cell and leaving messages, and then calling Marie's girlfriends, none of whom answered. Dad went into his tight-jawed self-control mode. When she finally got home, it was close to midnight. We heard Jon's bike pull up in front. Mom ran to the door, followed by me and Dad. She opened it just as Jon took off. Marie came up the walk carrying her book bag. She looked at the three of us standing in the doorway and said, "What?"

It wasn't the first time Marie had disappeared and come home late, so I knew the routine. Dad shook his head, made a sound with his lips that encompassed disgust, frustration, and resignation all in one exhalation. Mom was all, *Are you all right? Where have you been? Why didn't you answer your phone?*

Mom's questions quickly morphed into yelling. Marie started yelling back. Dad turned his back on them and went to bed. I listened to the yelling for a few minutes, then went to my own room and shut the door. The yelling would soon become crying, and the two of them would end up having a long mother-daughter talk in the kitchen.

It was always the same; nothing would change; it would happen again.

My family.

The next morning everything was back to what passes for normal. Dad left for work early so he wouldn't have to deal. Mom's eyes were all baggy and dark from the crying and no sleep. Marie was quiet and wouldn't look anybody in the eye. I tried to lighten the mood at the breakfast table by making a joke about Marie "studying late." Nobody laughed.

I asked Marie, "Is Jon picking you up this morning?"

"Mikey, shut up," she said.

Mom poured herself a cup of coffee and took it out to the patio.

"You are so lame," Marie said.

"I'm not the one who skipped school and came home at midnight."

"It was eleven thirty, and screw you."

"What happened to Jon's eye?"

She sat stirring her corn flakes, getting them good and mushy. After a while she shoved the bowl aside.

"He had a fight with his dad."

That wasn't what I had expected.

"His dad kicked him out. I had to help him move his stuff over to his brother's apartment."

"Jon has a brother?"

"Stepbrother, really. From Jon's mom's first marriage. He lives on Front Street, over on the east side."

That was all the way on the other side of the city. I

liked the idea of Jon living as far away as possible.

"Did you talk to him?"

"I was with him all day—what do you think?"

"I mean, did you talk to him about the money?"

Marie did her eye-roll thing. "It's always about *you*. Jon gets beat up and kicked out of his own house, and I get grounded, and all you can talk about is *your* pathetic problems."

"Did you talk to him or not?"

"No. It wasn't the right time. Besides, you lost his package; you should pay for it."

My sister.

Jon didn't show up at school again on Tuesday, and I let myself imagine that I would never see him again. Maybe now that he was living all the way across town he would transfer to another high school. So instead of looking over my shoulder all day, I made an effort to appreciate the educational system.

I made several sarcastic and amusing remarks during American Lit—we had just started reading *The Catcher in the Rye*, so it seemed appropriate for me to channel Holden Caulfield, the original wise-ass. Mr. Clemens was not appreciative, but he didn't send me to the office or anything.

After that I almost got kicked out of Biology for feeding Mr. Bush's pet rat a Cheeto, but I handed in my Cultural Studies report on time, and I made it through gym without getting snapped by a towel. After school I talked Shayne into going to Thriftway with me. He didn't seem all that excited about it, but he came.

Thriftway is my favorite used-clothing store. It's like a Goodwill, but they sell only clothing. Mrs. Jerdes, the owner, had set aside a hardly used bar mitzvah suit for me—an unusual dark green with pale blue pinstripes. Nineteen dollars. I tried it on. Perfect fit. I found Shayne back by the denim rack sorting through the black jeans.

"What do you think?" I said, holding my arms out and turning around.

Shayne looked me up and down.

"It's you, Mikey," he said.

Since I was enjoying the fantasy that Jon was permanently gone, I paid for it with my last twenty dollar bill.

My good day continued after Shayne dropped me off at home. Mom was making rice with pigeon peas and sausage, one of my favorites. Dad got home early from work and was out in the garage puttering with the busted pump from his fountain. Marie had come straight home from school for once and was doing her homework in the den. I went through the pockets of my new suit and found a folded-up hundred dollar bill in the watch pocket. I'd found money in thrift store suits before, but never a hundred.

It was a sign.

I went to school the next day, Wednesday, feeling pretty good about things, especially when I saw that Jon was once again absent. Maybe he'd dropped out permanently. I could get behind that.

Shayne didn't show up either, which surprised me because when he had dropped me off the night before he had said, "See you tomorrow."

But I wasn't worried. Yet.

After school I texted him and tried calling him a few times, but always got shunted over to voice mail. I would have gone to his house but I had no idea where he lived. Maybe he'd changed schools or moved. I should have been worried, but instead I got mad. Like, why didn't he at least call me?

Walking home, I heard the sound of a motorcycle coming up behind me. I turned, thinking it might be Shayne, but it wasn't. It was the other *djab*.

"Little Mikey," said Jon. His eye looked better, but you could still see he'd taken a good punch. He wasn't smiling, and that was even scarier than when he *was* smiling. "Happy Wednesday," he said.

I said, "I thought you moved."

"Not that far," he said. "You got my money?"

I didn't even hesitate. I reached into my pocket and pulled out the hundred dollar bill and handed it to him.

"Seen your friend lately?" he asked.

I shook my head.

He laughed and rode off.

That night I tried to talk to Marie, thinking she might know something. She told me she hadn't heard from Shayne since seeing him at school on Tuesday.

"What about Jon?"

"What about him?"

"Has he said anything about Shayne?"

"Not to me. Why?"

"Because I saw him on the way home. He took a hundred bucks off me. And he said something about Shayne. Like he knew something."

Marie looked at me for a long time, then said, "I thought you said you didn't have any money."

"I don't, now. Is Jon still staying with his brother?"

"As far as I know. He hasn't called since the day I helped him move."

Thursday morning. Still no Jon—the rumor was that he had dropped out—and no Shayne. Nobody knew what had happened to him. I tried not to care, but I couldn't think about anything else. I went back and forth from worried to mad. Finally, I decided to ask somebody who would know.

Back in grade school, Trey Worthington had been my

friend. He was a year older, so we were never super-close, but back in the fourth and fifth grades he had sort of looked out for me. We were like Lennie and George in that book *Of Mice and Men*. I was the little smart one, and Trey was the giant oaf who protected me. Naturally, I had to do some of his homework as a trade, but it was a win-win deal.

That friendship did not survive the transition to middle school, but we did have a history, so it wasn't completely crazy for me to start a conversation with Trey. The hard part would be to get him alone. I saw him at lunch, but he was sitting with Kyle Ness, who scared me almost as much as Jon did. I didn't have a chance to talk to him until later, when I caught him coming out of his Remedial English class.

"Hey," I said, stepping in front of him.

Trey stopped, which was good, since he outweighed me by more than most people weigh, period.

"What's happening?" I said, offering him a fist bump.

Trey frowned at my clenched hand, reached out one of his own paws, and clasped my fist. My hand completely disappeared, and I thought, *Uh-oh*. But instead of crushing my hand to jelly, Trey simply gave it a soft squeeze like a gorilla testing the ripeness of a banana, then he let go and walked around me.

"Trey, wait."

He didn't stop, but he slowed down. I ran to catch up to him.

"Trey, I have to ask you something."

"What?" he said.

"What happened to Shayne?"

Trey stopped. "What makes you think something happened?" he said.

"He's not in school."

"So?"

"Also, Jon said something."

"He did? What did he say?"

"He asked me if I'd seen Shayne, and then he laughed."

"Why don't you ask *him*?" The left side of his upper lip lifted—a look of disgust, but I couldn't tell if he was disgusted at me for being so gutless, or if it was something else.

I said, "Because every time I try to talk to Jon, he figures out a way to make me regret it."

Trey snorted. Or maybe it was a laugh. Or a sneeze.

"He shouldn't even be here," he said.

"Who?"

"Your friend. Shayne."

"Why?"

"Because he's trouble." Trey looked up. Kyle Ness was coming toward us. In a low voice, Trey said, "But that thing he did? Flipping me? That was cool."

Then Kyle was within earshot, Trey's face settled into its standard belligerent mask, and I *escabullirse*d.

By Friday I wasn't so much worried about Shayne as I was mad at him for disappearing. And I was thinking about how I was going to come up with the money to pay Jon next Wednesday. I could sell a bunch of my suits back to Thriftway. Mrs. Jerdes would probably pay me only about five bucks each. Or she might refuse to buy them at all, since the market for bar mitzvah suits was limited. I reviewed all my other sources of income. I had a box of comic books, but they weren't worth more than five or ten dollars total. Mrs. Garcia would pay me something . . . maybe she needed some help with her yard. I could sell my bike, which I hardly ever rode anymore. I could probably come up with a hundred by Wednesday, but then what? What about the next week?

I considered other strategies: running away, faking an illness, getting myself thrown in jail . . . my options were limited. I even thought about doing as Mémé had suggested and going to the authorities. What then? A slap on the wrist for Jon, at best, and then one day I would find myself in a painful and dark place, and realize that Jon had shoved my head up my butt.

I got home from school feeling bleak. The house smelled of tomato sauce. That meant pasta. I plunked down on the sofa and stared across the room at a painting of several people standing on a beach looking out over the ocean. Mémé had bought the painting in Haiti and given it to Mom and Dad as a wedding present. I wanted to be inside that painting right then, feeling warm sand between my toes, hearing the sound of waves rolling up the beach, smelling the salty, weedy, fishy scent of the Caribbean. Not that I'd ever been there. All I smelled at the moment was tomato sauce.

I heard voices coming from out back. I got up and looked outside. Shayne and Marie were out on the patio talking and drinking orange sodas. I felt a tiny surge of hope, but it lasted only a second because I remembered I was mad at him. I went out to join them.

"Hey," I said, making sure not to sound as if I was glad to see him.

Shayne smiled. Marie scowled. Barkie, who was sleeping at Shayne's feet, looked up and yipped. I sat down on the chaise.

"You weren't at school all week," I said. I meant it as a simple observation, but it came out whiny.

"I was under the weather," Shayne said. That sounded like something my dad would say.

"What does that *mean*?" I asked. "Under the *weather*? What weather?"

Marie rolled her eyes. "Mikey, why don't you grow up?"

I realized then that I was even madder than I'd thought. Mad at Shayne for disappearing, mad at Marie for being Marie, mad at both of them for being there in the backyard together without me.

"Grow up yourself," I said. Brilliant repartee.

Shayne said, "I should have called you, but my cell broke."

"You couldn't use another phone?" I hated the way my voice came out.

He looked straight into my eyes and said, "I'm sorry, Mike."

Not everyone knows how to apologize. Most people are flat-out terrible at it. But coming from Shayne, that simple, plain, direct statement—"I'm sorry"—was pure gold. Just like *that*, I wasn't mad anymore.

"Were you sick?" I asked.

"I had a little accident. No big deal."

Marie had this little smile on her face like she gets when she knows something I don't.

"What happened?" I asked.

"Nothing much. How about you? What happened with Jon on Wednesday?"

"You mean, did I pay him?"

"Yeah."

I spread my arms. "I'm here, aren't I? No missing limbs, no ugly bruises, not deceased. Of course I paid him."

Shayne said, "Oh. Okay." But it wasn't okay at all. I could see he was disappointed in me, I guess because I didn't stand up to Jon and let him smash my face in. He said, "Marie and I were just talking about the fountain your dad wants to build."

Fountain? How were we all of a sudden talking about a *fountain?*

"Where that big stump is," Shayne said. "He wants to dig up the stump and put a fountain there. An eight-foot stone basin with a single jet coming up in the center and a couple of spotlights for at night. But I was telling him about this fountain I saw in Texas with five copper goldfish all around the rim shooting water out of their mouths and different-colored spotlights on each one so it looked like they were each spouting a different color of water. It was really cool. More complicated to build, but your dad knows his stuff. I told him I'd help him."

I stared at him as if he had sprouted pink antlers. I said, "Are you kidding me? A *fountain?* Did you have a stroke or something?"

"I think it would be amazing."

"Amazingly *lame*," I said.

"Shut *up*, Mikey," Marie said.

"Shut up yourself."

Shayne looked from me to her and back again. He stood up, wincing a little. "I gotta go. See you later." He walked off.

"Call me!" I said as he rounded the corner of the house—and then I felt really stupid. *Call me?* What was I, a girl begging for a date? I looked at Marie. She was laughing silently.

"Shut *up*," I said.

Then I asked her if she knew what had happened to him.

She made me wait a good ten seconds before she answered.

"He's been in the hospital," she said.

"You ever tase anybody?" Shayne asked.

Rawls shook his head. Stun guns were available to all officers on the force, but he'd never carried one himself. It felt too much like cheating. Ninety-nine times out of a hundred, a good cop could keep the peace simply by talking. The cops who carried stunners, in his opinion, were all too quick to tase any drunk or druggie who got a little belligerent.

"You ever *been* tased?" Shayne asked.

"No, but I've seen it. It looks really unpleasant."

The kid's eyes lost focus for a moment. Rawls wondered what he was seeing.

"It's not so bad," Shayne said. "At first you don't know what's going on—like the electricity scrambles your brain. Your arms and legs go all limp and spazzy, and it hurts, but it doesn't last long."

"Who tased you?"

"After I dropped Mikey off that day, I stopped off at the Pump and Munch up on Freeman Street. You know how they got motorcycle parking around the side? I just went in to grab a soda. Anyway, I came out of the store around the side of the building and there was this guy sitting on a chopped Harley right next to my bike. An older guy, like in his thirties. He had one of those haircuts where it's shaved on the sides, but long on top and tied back in a skinny braid going halfway down his back. Looked like he had a long-tailed rat sitting on his head."

Rawls agreed. "World's ugliest hairstyle," he said.

"The guy was looking at my bike. He said, 'This your German piece a crap?'

"I told him it was my piece of crap. He looked past me and I turned to see Jon and his guys standing there. Jon had this thing in his hand. I didn't know what it was at first, and when I figured it out, I wasn't quick enough. Next thing I knew I was flopping around on the ground.

"Like I said, the getting tased part wasn't so bad—I probably could have got back up in a minute or so—but Jon and Kyle started kicking me. I didn't even try to fight back." He looked up at Rawls. "They say it's hard to hurt somebody who isn't fighting back. Most guys don't have it in them. That's why they say if you're taking a beating and there's no way to win, you should just curl up and do nothing."

"Who are *they*?" Rawls asked. "The people who say that."

"You know. Self-defense experts. Anyway, Jon is one of those guys who *does* have it in him. If Trey hadn't pulled him off me, I think he would have kept kicking until I was dead. I spent two days in the hospital. Two broken ribs, a concussion, and a bruised kidney. I told the doctor I fell down a flight of stairs. I don't think he believed me, but that's what he wrote on my chart."

"Why didn't you report it?"

"My word against theirs. Nothing would have happened, except maybe more of the same."

Rawls made a note. "You say Trey Worthington intervened?"

"Yeah ... well, after they'd been kicking me for a while. Look, I'm not here to make a complaint. None of that matters anymore."

Rawls set down his notebook. "If it doesn't matter, why are you telling me about it?"

The kid didn't say anything for several heartbeats. "Okay, it matters, only not the way you think."

"What do I think?" Rawls's stomach was growling. *Why doesn't this kid get to the point?*

"You think I should get to the point," the kid said.

Rawls blinked, taken aback by hearing his thoughts echoed.

The kid said, "The *point* is, they kicked the crap out of me, and I kind of went into this zone where even as it was happening, I was thinking that maybe beating me up would be enough for Jon, and he would leave me alone and maybe even cut Mikey a break. So I was telling myself, *Just get through this, and everything will be okay.* I was telling myself not to get mad, to let it go, to not try to get back at them."

"You were thinking all this while they were kicking you?"

"And after. In the hospital. And I kept thinking about that rat-head guy on the Harley, just sitting there watching the whole time."

"He wasn't involved?"

"Just watching. He was enjoying it. Almost like they were putting on a show for him."

Rawls said, "Kid—"

"My name is Shayne."

"*Shayne.* This story—what's left of it—are we talking another five or ten minutes, or should I order a pizza?"

The kid—*Shayne*—thought about that for what felt like a long time. Then he said, "I like pepperoni."

"Hospital?" I said.

"Yeah," Marie said. "You know—one of those big buildings you go to when you get hurt?"

I was not the only sarcastic person in our family.

"What hospital?"

"Saint Stephen's, I think."

"What happened to him?"

"He got in a fight. Jon and Kyle and Trey beat him up."

"He told you that?" I was offended on two levels. One, that Shayne hadn't told *me*, and two, that he *had* told *her*.

Marie smirked, then took pity on me and said, "Shayne didn't tell me. He said he had an accident on his bike, but I knew it wasn't true because I heard about what really happened from Kyle."

"You knew Shayne was in the hospital and you didn't tell me?"

"Kyle just told me about it this morning. Did you know Shayne went and talked to Jon's dad last week?"

"He mentioned it."

"That's what made Jon's dad kick him out. So Jon and Kyle and Trey decided to teach Shayne a lesson. Jon's brother was there too, over behind the Pump and Munch.

Then afterward they got scared that Shayne was going to die or something—I guess it was really bad—so nobody was saying anything. But when Shayne got released from the hospital last night, I guess Kyle decided it was okay to start bragging about it."

"Brag about it? Brag about how it took three of them?" I gave Marie a hard look, trying to figure out what was going on in her head.

She shrugged. "I just hope he doesn't try to get back at them."

"Shayne? What could he do?"

"I don't know, but I have a feeling he isn't going to let it go. I'm a little worried about him." For my sister, that was a remarkably sensitive thing to say.

After phoning in the order—half pepperoni and half veggie—Rawls walked down the hall to the front desk to tell Kramoski the pizza was coming and to give him some money to pay the delivery guy.

"Let me know as soon as it gets here. And grab a slice for yourself."

"Don't mind if I do. How's it going with that kid?"

Rawls shook his head. "I got no idea. He hasn't even said who he thinks he killed."

"Weird."

"Tell me about it."

"Throw him in the cage for a few hours. That'll loosen his tongue."

"His tongue's plenty loose. He's been talking the whole time. Like listening to *War and Peace*. But I still don't know what he came here to tell us."

Kramoski said, "Probably just looking for attention."

Rawls glanced back down the hall toward the interview room.

"Maybe," he said. "But I don't think so."

————

Back in the interview room, Shayne Blank, slumped in his metal chair, clanked the steel ring back and forth. He looked up when Rawls entered.

"About twenty minutes for the pizza," Rawls said.

The kid nodded.

"So, *Shayne*, you were saying you had a fight—"

"It was more like a stomping," Shayne said.

"Right." Rawls looked at his notes. "You got tased and stomped, and you spent a couple days in . . . which hospital?"

"Saint Stephen's."

Rawls wrote that down. Kramoski might be right about the kid making it all up. He could check with the hospital later to find out if any of this had ever really happened.

"Then what?"

"I laid low. You know, trying to think what I should do."

"What did you decide?"

"Like I said before, I pretty much decided to do nothing at all."

Rawls kept his face carefully neutral.

"I saw Mikey and Marie on Friday. I didn't tell them what happened. I didn't want to get them involved any more than they already were. Anyway, that older guy on the Harley?"

"The one who watched you get beaten," Rawls said.

"Yeah, him. I ran into him, kind of by accident, a couple days later. You know BG's Chop Shop?"

"Sure." BG's Chop Shop, a motorcycle supply and customizing business, was notorious. The owners, two former Hells Angels named Bunk and Griz, had been investigated several times for selling stolen parts, but nobody had ever made a case.

"I needed to replace the broken mirror on my bike, so I went over there and guess who was behind the counter. The Harley guy with the rat on his head. The guy that watched me get stomped."

Seeing the look Rawls was giving him, Shayne shrugged self-consciously. "I didn't know he worked there. It was completely a coincidence. But it was definitely the same guy. He didn't seem to recognize me. I showed him my busted mirror and he went in back to find a replacement. He came back with the new mirror a minute later. I said thanks, then asked him if he knew Jon Brande."

"'My little brother,' he said. 'Why?'"

"I said, 'Because that's who's paying for this mirror.' Then I left."

"He just let you walk off with the mirror?"

"Actually, he sort of chased me. He wasn't very fast."

"You stole the mirror."

"Technically."

"Is that right," Rawls said.

"I called the shop later. A guy named Griz answered the phone. I asked him who the guy was with the rat-tail hair. You ever hear of a guy named Wart Hale?"

Rawls felt his face and gut turn to wood.

"I think Wart is his nickname," Shayne said.

"Stewart Hale." Rawls forced himself to breathe normally. "His name is Stewart Hale. Wart for short."

"He seemed like a guy you might have run into."

"I met him when he was still in high school," Rawls said.

"Kind of a coincidence," Shayne said.

Rawls's thoughts went back nearly twenty years. He heard himself say, "I used to teach over at Gancy High. . . ."

"Where's that?"

"I forgot, you're not from around here. Gancy is on the south side."

"What did you teach?"

Rawls coughed out a bitter laugh. "Creative Writing and Parking Lot," he said.

"Parking Lot?"

Rawls nodded, wishing he hadn't mentioned it. The memories of his last days as a teacher were still painful. He had an unworthy thought then, which he cast off as quickly as it had arrived. But the ghost of the thought remained, like words scrawled on a steamed mirror.

The kid says he killed somebody. I hope it was Wart.

Shayne didn't call me all weekend, but he was back in school on Monday. To look at him you'd never know he'd been hospitalized just last week. But word spread quickly that Jon Brande and his friends had put the new kid in the hospital. By lunchtime even kids who had never heard of Shayne Blank knew what had happened.

Even though I still felt guilty for not knowing Shayne had been hurt and for assuming he'd somehow abandoned me, I was still mad at him for not telling me about what had happened. I felt left out; that was what it came down to. So when I joined him at lunch, I shifted right into sarcastic mode.

Shayne was prying open a plastic clamshell containing an egg salad sandwich.

"I can't believe you're going to eat that," I said. "Where'd you get it? The Pump and Munch?"

"Yeah. So?"

"So it's probably been sitting in their cooler for a month."

He sniffed the sandwich. "Smells okay." He took a bite and chewed thoughtfully. "Tastes okay."

"How come you didn't tell me?" I said.

"Tell you what?"

"That you got your ass kicked," I said.

He took another bite, chewed, and swallowed. "Because it was none of your business," he said.

"How is it not my business? I thought we were friends."

"We haven't known each other that long. I don't make friends that fast."

That was a kick in the gut.

"What*ever*." I said it as nastily as I could, but it didn't seem to bother him. He was looking across the lunchroom at Trey and Kyle.

"Jon's not in school," he said.

"Probably because he's scared to death of *you*."

"I doubt it." Taking me completely seriously.

"He wasn't here all last week," I said. "I think he dropped out. I can't say I'll miss him."

"Are you going to pay him again this week?"

"If I can find the money. Not that it's any of *your* business."

"You're absolutely right," Shayne said. "It's not my business. You *should* pay him. I should never have gotten involved."

I couldn't argue with that. So I didn't.

He was looking at Kyle and Trey. "There's no reason for me to drag you into my mess."

"How is it *your* mess?"

"Jon and I are like two freight trains on a collision course."

I looked at Trey and Kyle. "He has the bigger train," I said.

Shayne nodded slowly. "That doesn't change anything."

He gave me a frozen-faced look, as if he had suddenly grown an invisible, impermeable shell. "Don't take this personal, Mikey, but maybe we shouldn't hang out anymore." He got up, walked two tables over, and took an empty seat next to some sophomores.

I was floored. Did he just *unfriend* me? And what was that about *him* dragging *me* into his mess? If anybody had dragged anybody *anywhere,* it was Jon.

I almost got up and went after him, but then I decided, why bother. I finished my lunch alone, trying to act as if I was happy to be there. At one point I looked over at Kyle and Trey. Kyle was smirking at me; Trey stared glumly at Shayne.

27. RAWLS

During his first year at his first teaching job, twenty-six-year-old George Rawls had despised parking lot duty above all else. Because he was male, slightly larger than average, and the youngest teacher at Gancy High, he got stuck standing in the student parking lot every day after school let out. The kids called him Officer Rawls. He hated that. He had become a teacher so he could make a positive difference, educating and inspiring young people to become happy, productive adults. The last thing he wanted to be was a cop—even a fake parking lot cop.

The idea, according to the principal, was to "establish an adult presence" in the student lot. Keep them from lighting up, fighting, littering, or performing other forbidden acts, at least until they were safely off school property. Mostly the kids behaved because any infraction would lead to loss of parking privileges, at a minimum. Serious offenses—drug use, displaying a weapon, running over another student, et cetera—would result in automatic expulsion.

Day after day, Rawls would stand conspicuously near the parking lot exit, rain or shine, smiling and nodding like a bobblehead to each car full of chattering teens as they drove out of the lot and into their nonschool lives. So far that year he'd had little reason to invoke his authority—a few cigarette incidents, one shoving match between Allie Franson and Britt Hoades, and a minor fender bender. His presence acted as a deterrent, and that was exactly the point.

He knew, of course, that they were getting away with plenty. Sometimes Rawls would fantasize that he had X-ray vision and could see into every trunk and every glove compartment, and under every seat. Marijuana, alcohol, weapons—if he went through every car from bumper to bumper he'd find it all. But so long as they kept it under his radar, it was okay with him. If every kid got nailed for every violation, the school would be half-empty.

There were a few of them, however, who he would not have minded busting. The ones responsible for the harder drugs, especially. The weed and diet pills didn't bother him so much—after all, less than a year earlier he'd been in college, where such drugs were as ubiquitous as lattes and beer. But crack, meth, even opiates had started showing up recently, and those drugs were really messing with some of the kids. Dara Jensen, for example. Back in September she had been a cheerful, slightly plump junior. By December she had dropped twenty pounds, and she looked like a model. But by February she'd dropped another twenty pounds and looked more like a concentration camp victim. Some of Dara's friends were also losing weight rapidly.

It was hard for him to watch, and he had no idea how

to stop it—drugs were coming at these kids from every direction: from the streets, from older siblings and cousins, from their parents' medicine cabinets . . . but there were a few Rawls suspected of doing far more than their share in the pharmaceuticals trade.

One was Dev Donato, a classic stoner right out of *Fast Times at Ridgemont High*, complete with the red eyes, laid-back delivery, and general incomprehension of where he was and what was expected of him. Rawls had him pegged for selling weed—mostly because how else could the kid afford to stay high all day every day?

As for the harder drugs . . . there was Stewart Hale, known to his friends as Wart.

Rawls knew—though he could not have said exactly *how* he knew—that Wart was the go-to guy for the Gancy High drug users. Even back then, when he had never imagined himself as a cop, he had already possessed that cop sense. He supposed it was a combination of little things— who hung out with Wart; how the other students acted around him; the bits of expensive flash Wart liked to hang around his neck, wrists, and fingers; and that indefinable *something* about the way Wart carried himself. Like he had a secret, like he had power. But knowing that Wart was selling drugs and being able to stop him were two different things.

Besides, it wasn't his responsibility, so George Rawls, creative writing and parking lot specialist, just did his job and tried not to care too much. That was, until Dara Jensen stabbed Trish Gomez in the face with a scissors. The formerly sweet and shy sixteen-year-old had exploded during art class, leaving the Gomez girl with a four-inch gash down her left cheek. Dara wouldn't talk about it. That night she hung herself with her nylon fishnet stockings in a holding cell downtown. The autopsy revealed that Dara had been high on methamphetamine.

Thinking back to those events, Rawls tried to understand why he had done what he did. Dara Jensen had been nothing to him. Just another kid. As for Trish Gomez, he didn't even remember her face—or what was left of it.

Still, Rawls had taken it all very personally. He had seen Dara talking to Wart Hale on several occasions, and he was convinced—though he had no proof—that Wart had been supplying her with meth. Still, he might have done nothing, but the day after Dara died, he'd been driving past the McDonald's on South Front Street when he saw Wart hanging in the parking lot with a bunch of his friends. Something inside him snapped.

Rawls pulled into the parking lot, jumped out, and walked up to Wart, who regarded him with a smug, mildly questioning smirk. The smirk disappeared when Rawls grabbed Wart by the front of his shirt, slammed him against the side of his car so hard the window shattered, and screamed in his face. He didn't remember exactly what he had said, but there were words he never expected to hear himself utter to a student. He then threw Wart aside and began rummaging through the car, throwing the contents of the glove compartment onto the lot, emptying the center console, going through the trunk, and pulling up the back seats. He found nothing more incriminating than a half-empty pack of Marlboros and a few empty beer bottles. He turned away from the car to find the smirk had returned to Wart's face.

"Mr. Rawls, you have one too many cups of coffee today?"

At that moment, Rawls wondered if he was capable of murder. Wart must have wondered too, because he held up his hands and backed away, saying, "Easy, Mr. Rawls. I didn't do nothing!"

Rawls managed to stifle his rage, in part because he sensed that he was close to destroying his own life along with Wart's, and partly because the off-duty cop hired by McDonald's was running toward them with one hand on his baton. Fortunately the cop assumed that Wart was the troublemaker, and Rawls was able to get back into his own car and drive off, knowing as he made his way across town that he had messed up badly. Wart Hale could get him fired. All he had to do was make a complaint, and Rawls's career as a teacher would be over.

As it turned out, Wart Hale had something else in mind.

A buzzing cell phone startled Rawls from his reverie. How long had it been ringing? Seconds? Minutes?

It was Kramoski. "Pizza's here," he said.

A few minutes later, Shayne and Rawls were eating, Rawls working on the veggie half as the kid munched his way through the pepperoni. Neither of them was saying much.

Midway through his third slice, Shayne asked Rawls if he had any kids.

Rawls shook his head.

"How come?" Shayne asked.

"Just never got around to it, I guess," said Rawls.

But he was thinking about Wart Hale.

Rawls had been surprised when Wart hadn't gone straight to the police or the school administration. He'd spent the next couple of days expecting a phone call or a hand on his shoulder: *Mr. Rawls, we've received a complaint . . .*

But Wart didn't do that. Instead, three days after the incident, Rawls looked out his classroom window to see several policemen going through his car. He put one of the students in charge of the class and ran outside. Moments later, Rawls was in handcuffs.

The police had discovered half a kilo of marijuana in his trunk, along with a broken, blackened crack pipe and several empty prescription bottles with labels that read Vicodin, Adderall, and oxycodone.

All he could say was, "I've never seen this stuff before," and, "What were you doing searching my car?"

Not that there was any question in his mind—the drugs had been planted there by Wart Hale, and it was Wart who had made the anonymous call to the police.

Rawls had spent the night in jail. The next day, bailed out by his lawyer, Rawls learned that the marijuana was of such poor quality that it was worthless on the drug market, but that didn't make it any less illegal. Wart had used a bad batch of pot to frame him.

Eventually, Rawls and his lawyer were able to convince the police to investigate further. They found that Rawls's fingerprints appeared nowhere on the bagged drugs or paraphernalia. They found no trace of drugs in his home. And they located a witness—a student named Stephanie Kelso—who had seen two boys break into Rawls's car and throw something into his trunk. She could not—or would not—name them.

Rawls was cleared of all charges, but when he returned to school, the principal took him aside and told him that the school had received a complaint from a student— Rawls did not have to ask who—about the altercation at the McDonald's. The student's story had been corroborated by the off-duty cop working there.

"If you leave now, none of this will go on record," the principal said. He didn't seem angry, just sad and tired.

"I just wanted to make a difference," Rawls said. It was all he could do to keep from bursting into tears.

The principal, who was not a bad man, said, "I'm doing you a favor, son. Find another way to make a difference. And learn to control your temper."

Two months later, Rawls had registered at the university with a double load of classes in criminology. By the end of the following year he had joined the police force.

Rawls pointed at the last remaining slice of veggie pizza. "Help yourself," he said.

Shayne picked up the slice, took a bite, made a face, and set it back in the box. "Olives," he said.

"You don't like olives?"

Shayne shook his head.

"You were telling me about stealing a mirror," Rawls said.

"Oh yeah, the mirror. It fit on my bike just fine."

Rawls waited.

Shayne said, "Okay, it was sort of an impulsive thing to do."

"You think? Jon had already beat the hell out of you. Why would you want to make him any angrier?"

"He broke my mirror."

"I thought you said it was the other kid, Trey."

"Trey did it because of Jon. Look, I'm not saying it was smart for me to take off with the mirror, but guys do stupid stuff when they get mad. You ever do anything stupid?"

Rawls thought about losing it that day in the McDonald's parking lot.

"Never," he said.

29. MIKEY

It wasn't just me that Shayne decided to unfriend. The next day he unfriended Marie, too.

I passed them in the hall that afternoon. Marie was firing all her guns—playing with her hair, batting her eyes, licking her lips, the whole package—but Shayne had on his impenetrable, invulnerable, hard-eyed face, the same look he'd used on me at lunch. It gave me a little boost to see Marie about to get the same treatment.

At the end of the day, right as I was leaving school, I saw Marie in the parking lot by the motorcycles, talking to Kyle. Shayne, whose bike was parked a few spaces down, walked right past them. Marie never looked his way. She knew he was there—Marie's guydar is practically a superpower—but she pointedly ignored him. Shayne got on his bike and sat there. Marie went into her hair-flipping, lip-licking routine with Kyle. It was all for Shayne—Marie was not interested in Kyle. But a few seconds later she climbed onto the back of Kyle's bike and rode off with him. Shayne watched them until they turned out of sight, then started his bike and headed in the same direction.

Apparently, although he had unfriended Marie, he still cared what happened to her.

Even then, in the midst of my feeling sorry for myself and resentful and angry and all the other negative crap that goes on along with being told to get lost, I understood what Shayne thought he was doing.

He thought he was protecting us.

I took the long way home and found myself walking past Pépé and Mémé's place, so I stopped by for a visit. Pépé immediately got out the checkerboard. Mémé was lying down with a headache, so I didn't get bombarded with food, but that was okay. I really just wanted to ask Pépé about *djabs*. I waited until we were several moves into the game.

"I've been thinking about what you said, about *djabs*," I said.

"That was just an old man talking," he said.

"Yeah, but it kind of made sense."

Pépé pushed one of his pieces forward, offering me a jump. I examined the board carefully. If I jumped him, he would get a double jump and have one potential king on my side of the board. I tried to think it out, then saw how I could advance another piece and force him to make a jump that would set me up for a triple.

I made the move. Pépé grinned.

"Wondered if you'd see that," he said, resignedly making the move.

I said, "Do you think people are like checkers?"

"No." He sat back in his chair. "I think checkers are like people."

"What's the difference?"

"People came first."

I made my triple jump. "King me."

Pépé kinged me.

"These boys you know," he said. "They are just boys. Not checkers. Not *djabs*. You should stay away from them, even the one who takes your side."

"No problem there. He doesn't want to be friends anymore."

"You see? A *djab* would not give up."

"I didn't say he's given up. I think he doesn't want to be my friend because he thinks it'll make problems for me."

"Maybe he is right."

"Yeah, but why would he do that?"

"That is one thing you don't know—what is in another person's head. What of the other boy?"

"He still thinks I owe him money."

"That is not good." Pépé moved a piece forward. "Your mémé may be right. Maybe you should talk to your teachers."

"Jon hasn't been in school. I think he dropped out."

"Then the police."

I imagined myself walking into the police station. What would they do? Nothing. I had no proof of anything, just accusations.

Pépé watched me, as if following my thoughts.

He said, "Your move."

I looked down at the board. He was offering me another jump. I concentrated for a long time, thinking ahead, until I understood every possible way the game could go for the next three moves. Pépé waited patiently. The problem was that while I had figured out how to make that triple jump two moves earlier, Pépé had been thinking even further ahead, and all of a sudden things didn't look so good for me.

I finally looked up and said, "I have no good moves."

Pépé nodded. "That happens sometimes."

Marie didn't make it home for dinner that night. We had chicken with rice and peas, which normally I like, but it was hard to enjoy with all the vibes coming off my folks. Mom was all small-mouthed and jittery and silent, eating her food with small bites and chewing them to death. Dad tried to compensate by complimenting her on the food, then going on and on about his plans to build a new fountain in the backyard. Neither of them mentioned Marie's name the whole time. I tried to lighten the mood by saying, "Isn't this nice, just the three of us!" The mood did not get lighter. In fact, Dad quit talking and his jaw started pulsing.

Later, I was in the living room trying to finish *The Catcher in the Rye* when I heard a motorcycle pull up. It was nine thirty—not an unreasonable time, even for a school night—except that Marie had promised to come straight home from school every day and not go out for a month. I put down the book and waited for the drama to reboot.

I could see the front entryway from where I was sitting.

Dad was the first to appear—he'd heard the motorcycle too. A few seconds later the door opened and Marie stepped inside. Dad didn't say anything. Marie looked up at him with the same stubborn expression she had perfected at age four. She didn't say anything either, at first. Then, after a few seconds that felt like minutes, she spoke.

"Well? Are you going to hit me, or what?"

Dad's face almost broke. He said, "Marie . . ."

"You're all pathetic!" She walked around him and started up the stairs, but ran into Mom halfway up and the screaming commenced.

It was pretty intense. Dad fled to the den and turned on the TV. Marie and Mom went at it right there on the stairs, yelling back and forth. I was starting to think I'd have to climb up the gutter to get to my bedroom, but after a few intense minutes of back-and-forth, Marie got past Mom and stomped off to her room and slammed the door.

Mom went into what I call her dry-cry mode, tight-faced and breathing loudly through her nose and slamming things around, as she cleaned the kitchen. I tried to finish my book but Holden Caulfield was really starting to piss me off with all his whining. I tossed the book aside with the last thirty pages unread, went up to Marie's room, and knocked on the door.

"Go away!" she yelled.

I kept knocking, one knock every five seconds, which is really irritating and impossible to ignore. About ten knocks later the door opened and Marie looked out.

"What?" she said. Her eyes were red. I couldn't tell if it was from crying or dope.

"Are you okay?" I asked.

She dragged her sleeve across her eyes. "Why wouldn't I be okay?"

"I don't know. I just . . . are you going out with Kyle now?"

"Kyle?" She unleashed a high-pitched, hysterical laugh. "You must be joking."

"I just wondered because you rode off with him."

"He took me over to Jon's." She backed away and sat down on her bed, leaving the door open. I was surprised— the number of times Marie had invited me into her room was, I think, zero. I stepped through the door cautiously. Nothing happened. She didn't start screaming at me. Her room was a disaster area, as usual. Clothes everywhere, utter chaos. The exact opposite of my room.

I sat down on the only chair, the one in front of her vanity.

Marie said, talking really fast, "Jon's brother has a really cool place. This old apartment building that they made into like condos and he has roof access so he's got it set up like for parties with a big grill and tables and chairs and stuff like a huge patio in the sky. Tracy and Maura were there and a couple of Wart's friends—sort of creepy—and Wart's girlfriend, Greta. She was cool. We were on the roof. Did I say that already?"

"Who's Wart?" I couldn't get over the fact that my sister was talking to me, but it was weird how fast she was talking. I wondered which drug—or drugs—she'd been taking.

"Jon's brother. Stepbrother. It's short for Stewart. Wart is. He's like a biker. He has a Harley in his living room. So cool."

"What's Wart like?" I pictured a guy with an incredibly ugly lump for a head.

"He's okay." She began picking at a small scab on the back of her hand. "A little scary. Not like he *did* anything, but he seemed kind of tense. He wasn't mean to me, but he treated Jon like his slave. You know: 'Grab me a beer. Do this. Don't do that. Clean that up.' I think he's pissed that Jon had to come and live with him—probably why he made us all leave so early—but he likes having somebody to order around. He ordered Jon around a lot." She managed to lift off the scab; a bead of blood formed. She stared at it, fascinated.

"Are you *sure* you're okay?" I asked her.

Her eyes flicked to me, then back to the bead of blood. "'Course I am. I'm just, I'm just a little wound up because of Mom being such a bitch and all. And school tomorrow, I don't have my Psychology paper done, all my jeans are in the wash, did you know Tracy got a kitten? It's so-o-o-o-o cute."

I was sure she was high on something, but I knew if I said so she'd deny it, so I just let her go on about Tracy's kitten for a while, then circled back to Jon and his brother.

"Is it permanent? Is Jon going to stay with his brother from now on?"

"He's working for Wart now. I mean, I guess he always was but now it's like full time on account of Wart is spending most of his time at BG's and since Jon's done with school now he has more time—"

"Wait—Jon's officially dropped out?"

"The only reason he was going at all was because his dad made him and now he's kicked out so . . ."

"Did you see Shayne?" I asked.

She pushed her hair back. She had forgotten about the drop of blood on her hand; it left a red streak across her cheek. "He gave me a ride home," she said.

"He did? *Shayne* was *there?*"

"Tracy and I were leaving, and he just happened to be driving by."

"He followed you and Kyle when you left school," I said.

"He did?" She leaned forward. "Really?"

"Maybe he just happened to be going in the same direction."

"He's a total prick, anyway. I tried to talk to him this morning and he blew me off, like he's too cool or something. And when he gave me a ride home I thought he'd say he was sorry or something but he just dropped me off and he was like, *later*. Do you think I'm fat?"

"I . . . huh? No, you're not fat at all."

She stuck out her foot. "I think I have fat ankles."

I didn't want to get into a discussion of her ankles, so I said, "Shayne blew me off too. I think he just doesn't want to make problems with Jon. You know, because Jon's mad at him and he doesn't want it to rub off on us."

"Jon could care less about Shayne."

"Did he say anything about me?"

"Who? Shayne?"

"Jon."

"No. Why would he?"

"Because I'm supposed to pay him a hundred bucks, that's why."

"Oh. I wouldn't worry about it. He's really busy now. Wart has him making deliveries all over town."

"Delivering what?"

"What do you think?"

"You mean his dope?"

She shrugged. "Duh."

I said, "Jon's brother is a drug dealer, too?"

"Where do you think Jon gets it?"

"Are you on something?"

She shrugged again, rediscovered the small wound on the back of her hand, licked it, wiped her hand on her jeans, then looked up at me.

"Are you still here?"

That night I lay in bed tossing and turning, and every time I closed my eyes I saw patterns of black and red checkers. I could hear Marie in her room—little scraping, clunking, squeaking, shuffling noises that went on for hours. I imagined a massive drawer reorganization or maybe a search for a lost earring. I didn't get to sleep until after three. Marie was still going strong.

"I followed Kyle and Marie downtown to this apartment building. I waited until they went inside, then I went into the lobby and checked the mailbox. There was a 'Stewart Hale' in apartment 401, up on the top floor. I figured that had to be Wart. I bought a cappuccino at the coffee shop across the street and sat at one of the outside tables and watched the apartment building. I sat there for a long time. I had to buy, like, three coffees.

"Around sunset, Wart pulled up on his Harley with a woman on the back. A little later I heard music and saw Marie up on the roof, looking down over the edge. She didn't see me. Every now and then I could see other people up there when they got close to the edge. I thought about just going up there, like, 'Hey, I heard you guys were having a party!' But that would have been stupid."

"I thought that was your specialty," said Rawls.

Shayne looked at him curiously. "My dad used to say that," he said.

"Used to?"

"I haven't seen him in a while."

Neither of them spoke for a few seconds. Shayne

flopped the steel ring back and forth a few times, then withdrew his hands to his lap.

"Actually, I didn't know what to do. Originally I just wanted to make sure Marie was all right. And I guess I was curious about where they were going. I saw Trey come out a little later and get on his bike, so I went over to talk to him. He was surprised to see me. I asked him what was going on. He said, 'Nothing.' I asked him what they were doing up there and he sort of shrugged, almost like he was embarrassed. Then he said, 'Partying.'

"'You mean getting high?' I asked.

"He shrugged again and said, 'What else?'

"I said, 'You don't get high?'

"He said, 'Not like *that*.' Then he started his bike and took off.

"I wasn't sure what was going on upstairs—I mean, if they were shooting heroin or smoking crack or whatever. I decided to hang around. Just in case, you know?"

Rawls didn't know, but he nodded anyway.

"A couple hours later, Marie came out the front door with Tracy Linnell, one of her girlfriends from school. They seemed to be walking okay. Kind of jittery, maybe, not like they were drunk or anything. They went down the sidewalk to a yellow Volkswagen. Tracy got in on the driver's side. I jumped on my bike and pulled up alongside. Marie hadn't gotten in the car yet. She was standing on the other side waiting for Tracy to unlock the door.

"Tracy rolled down her window and gave me that look like girls do when they're being tough—like you're the least interesting person on earth. 'What do *you* want?' she said. I ignored her and looked over the top of the car at Marie and asked her if she needed a ride home.

"She said, 'I got a ride home.' She was kind of twitchy.

"I asked Tracy if she was the official designated driver.

"She said, 'What are you, some kind of junior cop?'

"I told her I was going by Marie's anyway and just thought she might need a lift. Marie stuck her head in the car and they had a girl conference. Then Marie stepped back and Tracy screeched out of her parking space, almost knocking me over. Marie watched her go, then looked at me, like, *now* what? Because I'd more-or-less told her that I didn't want anything to do with her, and I guess I should have stuck with that because just as she was climbing on the back of my bike, Jon and Kyle came out of the building and started toward us. They must have seen me from the roof. I took off."

"Did they come after you?" Rawls asked.

"I don't think so. They couldn't have caught up with me anyway."

"Then what did you do?"

"I dropped Marie off at home."

Rawls waited for him to say more, but Shayne just sat there staring at nothing, rubbing the steel ring with his thumb.

Rawls silently counted to thirty, then said, "I assume there's more to your story."

"Just a little," said Shayne.

31. MIKEY

I don't know what time Marie got to sleep, but in the morning she was impossible to get out of bed. Mom tried spraying her with a plant mister, but Marie burrowed into her covers, yelling why didn't everybody just leave her the hell alone. That was fine with me; I took off for school.

First hour, Shayne was quiet, as always, hiding deep inside himself but alert. We exchanged a nod when our eyes met during first period, but neither of us said anything. I knew we wouldn't be eating lunch together.

I don't know how the drama at home ended, but Marie finally showed up at school around second period, looking like crap—hair all bed-head in back, lipstick crooked, and a ridiculous amount of makeup around her eyes. That was unusual for Marie, who usually spent a lot of time putting herself together every morning.

I had eighty-two dollars in my pocket. It was Wednesday. Jon wasn't in school, of course, but I figured I should have some money with me just in case. I'd been thinking about Pépé and his checkers, and he was right. People are not like checkers, but checkers *are* like people. I was also thinking about Shayne saying that he and Jon were like two trains about to collide. That fit with the checkers thing—in checkers, you have to keep moving forward. There's no going back until you get kinged, and what comes next is a checkers' bloodbath.

I ran into Tracy Linnell in the hall—she didn't look much better than Marie. I asked her how her new cat was doing.

"His name is Jumpy," she said. Her eyes were puffy and red, and she'd chewed off most of her lipstick. "How'd you know I had a cat?"

"Marie told me."

"Oh. He's fine. He jumps on my face in the middle of the night. By the way, your sister is hogging the nurse bed."

"What's a nurse bed?"

"The bed in the nurse's office. I tried to go in there but she was hogging it."

That explained why I hadn't seen Marie all afternoon. She'd gone to the school nurse and told her she had a migraine or cramps, and the nurse had let her crash for a while.

The last hour of the school day, I spent the whole class thinking about all the routes I could take to get home— the idea being to avoid running into Jon. I finally decided to take the number 17 bus, which would drop me off on Harrold Avenue. From there I could take Ninth Street back home. Anyway, that was the plan, but when the final chime announced the end of the school day and I joined the mass exodus, I stopped at the front doors. Students bumped and jostled past me, a steady stream pushing through the glass doors and spilling down the shallow steps to the buses.

Jon Brande was sitting on his bike at the curb, between the student parking and the buses, watching the entrance.

I stayed inside, standing well back from the glass doors. A few minutes later Kyle rolled up beside Jon with Maura Dansky riding behind. Several students of the stoner variety stopped to pay homage to Jon. Marie walked past me and pushed through the doors and trotted down the steps toward him. She had cleaned herself up a bit. Her hair looked normal and she had her lipstick on straight. Jon waved her over. They talked. Jon pointed at the school. I knew he couldn't see inside, but it felt as if he was stabbing his finger straight at me. Marie shook her head, then shrugged and walked back to the school and entered the now empty—except for me—foyer. She said, "Jon says for you to come talk to him."

"Tell him I already left."

"He won't believe me."

"Tell him you couldn't find me."

"He knows when I'm lying."

"Tell him I'll pay him in a few days."

"He just wants to talk to you."

"I don't think so," I said.

I felt a presence. We both did, because Marie and I turned our heads at the exact same time. Shayne was standing a few feet away, looking at us with that alert, cloaked expression.

"Everything okay?" he said.

Marie gave him a scathing look and said, "What do you care?" She shoved the door open and trotted down the steps. She stopped at the bottom, looked back at us, then walked over to where Jon was waiting.

Shayne said, "What's with her?"

I repeated what Marie had said. "What do you care?" I pushed open the door and walked slowly down the steps toward Jon Brande. He didn't see me coming at first, and then he did. His lips drew back from his teeth and formed a smile. He climbed off his bike and stood with his back to it, leaning against the seat. I kept walking toward him, feeling Shayne's eyes on my back, having no idea what I was about to do or say.

Jon held up his hand, palm forward. "High five, little dude!"

I would have had to jump to reach his hand. I wasn't going to do that.

"You wanted to see me?" I said.

Jon lowered his hand but kept the grin. "It's Wednesday, Mikey."

"That's very good," I said. "And tomorrow's Thursday."

Jon's smile lost a few watts. "'Scuse me?" he said.

I didn't look away, even though deep inside I was screaming scared. My mouth didn't care. My mouth said, "Was that all you wanted? To tell me what day it is?"

I was very impressed with my mouth, even though it was trying hard to get me killed.

His smile went away altogether. "You owe me," he said.

"I owe you nothing. Even if I had it, I wouldn't pay you another dime."

Too astonished to reply, Jon looked at Kyle and at Marie, checking to see if they'd heard it too. Kyle had a faint crooked smile—he probably saw it as a good excuse for a stomping. Marie just looked scared. A few other students were watching, but keeping their distance.

There was about six feet between us. Jon took a step toward me. I didn't back away, to both of our surprise.

"Go ahead, do it," I said. "Show everybody how tough you are." Jon Brande's scowling, reddening face looked unreal to me. I imagined him as an overgrown toddler working up a massive temper tantrum, and that made me smile.

"You think something's funny?" His fists were clenched white.

Kyle put a hand on Jon's shoulder. "Dude."

Jon shrugged him off. "What?"

"Look."

Jon looked past me. With a visible effort, he unclenched his fists and took a step back. I turned to see Mr. Peterson, the assistant principal, standing on the steps watching us. Off to the side, leaning against the building with his arms crossed, stood Shayne. Jon looked from one to the other. He got on his bike, started it, and made a head motion to Marie. She climbed on behind him, giving me an *are-you-out-of-your-mind* look. I was wondering the same thing.

"We'll talk later, Mikey," Jon said. *"Later."*

I watched him ride off, followed by Kyle and Maura. When I looked back at the school, Mr. Peterson was still there.

Shayne was gone.

What did I expect? That Shayne would run up and congratulate me for standing up to Jon? That Jon would be frightened off by my sudden display of fearlessness? That my dad would hear about me standing up for myself and look at me with pride, for once? That I would get an immediate testosterone-driven growth spurt?

Well, yeah, I guess I expected a little bit of all those things. The same way you buy a lottery ticket and expect it to be a winner. Even though you know it probably won't be, there is always a chance. A small chance. Very small.

My bus pulled away from the curb. I would have to walk home.

With any luck at all, Jon would be on his way across town to his brother's place. How had my luck been running lately? Not so great.

I started walking. About half a block ahead of me I saw a figure walking with a rubbery, high-kneed gait, as if the sidewalk was paved with six inches of foam. It could only be the perpetually wasted Carlos Reye, one of Jon's best customers. I caught up with him as we were coming up to Thirty-third Street.

"Hey, Carlos," I said as I passed him.

Carlos stopped and looked at me, drawing back a little as if I had popped into existence from some other dimension.

"Whoa, hey, little suit dude!" He peered at me closely. His eyes were red, his pupils dilated. "You are, like *intense!*"

"Yeah, that's me. Mr. Intense."

Carlos thought that was the funniest thing he had ever heard. I waited for him to stop giggling, then asked him if he'd talked to Jon lately.

"Jon, yeah, he's like living across town with some scary biker dude."

"Is he still dealing the same stuff as always? Weed and X?"

Carlos had to think about that for a few seconds. "I guess. Only he's more into ups lately."

"Ups?"

"*Andale andale, arriba! Yee-ha!*" Carlos started laughing so hard there was stuff coming out of his nose. I tried to make sense out of what he had just said, but failed.

"What is *andale?*" I asked.

"You don't know *andale?* I thought you were Mexican."

"You have me confused with yourself," I said.

"Wow. Dude. That is *intense.*"

Talking to Carlos was giving me an unpleasant contact high. This must be what it's like to make first contact with an intelligent alien. Except for the intelligent part.

"So what's with the *andale?*" I asked.

"That's what Speedy Gonzales used to say."

"Who is Speedy Gonzales?"

"Dude! You don't watch cartoons? Speedy's like this really fast mouse."

"Speedy . . ." I said. "You mean Jon's dealing speed now?"

"Speed, crank, it's messed up, man. I don't mess with it myself. I mean—" He grinned. "I'm already seeing leprechauns in suits." He cracked up again.

He was still giggling when I walked off.

Shortly after Leon Sullivan's rooftop freak-out, we spent one whole period in Mr. Wiseman's Health class talking about methamphetamine, also known as meth, crank, crystal, speed, glass, and I-don't-know-how-many other names. Basically, it's a Godzilla version of Adderall. According to Mr. Wiseman, it can turn you into a raving psychotic addict overnight.

Mr. Wiseman has been known to exaggerate.

"So why do people do it?" I asked him.

Mr. Wiseman told us one of the most common reasons is because meth is not only the Godzilla of amphetamines, it is also the Godzilla of diet drugs. It pumps up the metabolism almost to the point of heart failure and completely kills the appetite.

I could see a few of the girls in class perk up at that. But then Mr. Wiseman went on to describe the other effects, and when he got to the teeth-falling-out, foul-breath, terminal-acne part, those same girls seemed to lose interest.

I was thinking about that as I walked toward home. Thinking about Marie. I was thinking so hard I didn't even hear the motorcycle pull up behind me.

———

"Need a ride?"

My heart stopped a millisecond before I recognized Shayne's soft, edgy voice.

"You scared the crap out of me," I said.

"Sorry. You okay?"

"You mean except for having to worry about Jon every second of the day? Yeah, I'm just great."

"You don't have to worry about Jon today—he's over at his brother's place."

"How do you know that?"

"I followed him to make sure he wasn't hanging out around here, waiting for you. I don't know what you said, Mikey, but I think you pissed him off stupendously."

"It was probably a stupid thing to do."

"Probably," Shayne agreed. "Hop on. I'll buy you one of those high-octane coffee drinks."

"You're re-friending me?"

"I never *unfriended* you."

Shayne took off so fast I almost flew off the back of the bike. He leaned hard into the corners, wove in and out of traffic, and took an illegal shortcut through the Walgreens parking lot. When we got off at the Starbucks, I was a little shaky.

"Drive fast much?" I said.

"It helps me think."

"Or not think."

"That too."

We went in and ordered drinks. It's not on the menu,

but they will make a double-triple venti cappuccino if you ask. I asked. Shayne ordered a decaf latte. Sort of wimpy, but I didn't say anything because he was paying. When we sat down he started talking right away.

The first thing he said was, "Look, Mikey, I'm sorry."

"Sorry for what?"

"Everything. I'm afraid all I did was shove a stick in a hornets' nest."

"What difference does it make to you?"

Shayne sat without speaking for a long time, then he said, "Remember that day I met you?"

"It was only like the week before last."

"You know how come we got to be friends?"

"I can't even keep track of whether we're friends or not."

"Yeah, well, it's confusing, because I'm not actually here."

"You look here to me."

"I'm here now, but I'm not here for long. I'm just passing through. I mean, I won't be living here for years or anything. Because of my situation."

"What situation is that?"

"With my parents and all."

"Your doctor-soldier-spy whatever parents from Afghanistan-Australia-Africa-whatever?"

He waved his hand, as if to erase all that. "It doesn't matter. The point is, I hadn't planned on making any friends at all here, but I figured it was safe to hang out with you because you seemed like . . . uh, don't take this wrong, but you seemed like kind of a dink."

I stared at him in shock. "A *dink?*" I said.

"Like somebody I wouldn't like. Wouldn't miss. See, if I didn't make any friends here, didn't get involved, then it would be easy to leave. But then I got to like you. You're an okay guy once you get past the suit and the sarcastic mouth." He grinned.

"What's wrong with my suits?"

"Well, they sort of give the impression that you think you're special."

"I *am* special, to me. But that's not why I wear them."

"I know that now. You wear them for the same reason gang members wear colors, the same reason girls wear makeup, the same reason Jon rides a bike that's too big and too fast for him."

I didn't get that at all.

"For protection," he said. "It's like psychological body armor."

"That's ridiculous," I said. But I knew he was right. I always felt safer when I was wearing a suit. Like it would protect me.

He took a sip of his latte.

"Did you really think I was a *dink?*" I asked.

He shrugged. "Something like that."

"What you should have done, you should have picked Jon for a fake friend."

"I tried, that day in the cafeteria. It didn't take."

We stared at each other over our coffees, then both burst into laughter.

"You're kind of a dink too," I said.

"I know."

We laughed again, then Shayne suddenly sobered and leaned forward.

"I like your sister, too," he said.

"Marie?"

"You have more than one sister?"

"Not the last time I checked."

"I think she's in trouble. Because of me."

"She was a mess before she met you."

"I made it worse."

I saw something then in Shayne that surprised me: He had an ego the size of Jupiter.

I said, "It must be hard to be responsible for everything that happens."

He nodded, taking me seriously.

"That was supposed to be sarcastic," I said.

"Oh." He got it then.

I said, "Let me tell you about Marie."

33. MIKEY

"My dad used to drink," I said. "He'd come home from work and have a couple scotches. Sometimes three or four. That was okay—it just made him all smiley and jokey. He was actually kind of fun. Then, at dinner, he'd start drinking wine. My mom would have maybe one glass; Dad would drink the rest of the bottle.

"And then he would get mean."

"You mean like physical?"

"Not at first. The kind of mean he got was more like he'd start staring at one of us, like he'd look at me and say, 'You look like crap.' And then he'd go on to list everything he didn't like about the way I looked—my shirt was dirty, my mouth was hanging open, my hair was wrong, I was too short . . . always getting my height in there somehow. He was always telling me to 'man up.' How was I supposed to man up? I was only twelve years old. Or he'd go after my mom: *You used to have a nice figure—why don't you get off your fat butt and start exercising? You used too much oregano in the sauce.*

"Little stuff mostly, but he was relentless. It was like being pecked to death. Marie got it worst of all: *Get that hair out of your face—you look like a slut. What boy would look at you twice? You're going to be as fat as your mother. Sometimes I wonder if you're really my daughter.* And that was back when she was in the eighth grade. One time he called her 'nothing but a whore waiting to happen.'

"It got worse and worse. After a while he would come home with a few drinks in him already and start in on the scotch. That was when it started to get physical. At first it was like he'd give Mom a slap on the butt, like he was being playful, but you could see it hurt. And he would give me and Marie what he called dope slaps on top of the head, but really hard. Then one day Mom came down to breakfast with a big bruise on her cheek and Dad was being super-nice to her and she wouldn't talk to any of us.

"The next day he came home drunk again and took his scotch into the den and turned the TV up loud and didn't hear Mom when she called us for dinner. He finally came out halfway through dinner and started yelling at Mom about why hadn't she called him. He grabbed a plate and filled it with food and said he was going to eat his dinner out on the patio.

"My mom—I was really proud of her—as soon as he went outside, Mom locked all the doors."

"What did he do?" Shayne asked.

"He freaked. He started screaming at us and banging on the door and running around the house trying to pry open windows. All the neighbors came out to see what was going on. One of them called the cops when Dad smashed the glass in the patio door with a shovel. He cornered Mom in the kitchen and started slapping her. Marie was screaming—I think I was screaming too. Mom got away and ran outside, and he followed her and grabbed her hair and threw her on the ground. That was when the cops showed up. They tried to calm him down but he took a swing at one of them so they arrested him for assault. He spent the night in jail. They said my mom could press charges, but she wouldn't. He hasn't had a drink since."

"He just quit?"

"Yeah. I think it really scared him what he had done. One thing about my dad: When he decides to do something, he does it. He didn't go to treatment or AA or anything. The drinking stopped, he always got home from work at the same time, he complimented my mom on her appearance, and he took care of chores around the house right away, never letting them pile up. And he stopped criticizing me and Marie. He turned into this perfect, flawless, model father. In a way, it was even worse than when he was drinking."

"How so?"

"You ever live with someone who's trying to be perfect? Believe me, it sucks. Every time I did anything wrong— anything I knew would bug him—I'd look at him and he wouldn't say anything. His jaw would get tight, and I could hear in my head all the things that would have spilled out of him if he'd had a few drinks. And I could see how it pained him to hold it all in, so I'd feel doubly guilty for making him hurt. He's relaxed some in the past year or so. Mom says he's been on a 'dry drunk,' and it's taken him this long to find his new 'normal.' Things are better now, but he's still pretty tensed-up."

I'd never talked to anyone about the whole Dad thing before. I felt as if my brain had just taken a long overdue crap.

Shayne said, "I like your dad. He's kind of like my dad."

"Your dad's an ex-drunk?"

"No, but he had some bad things happen to him in the service, and he holds a lot of it inside." Shayne's eyes softened, then snapped back into focus. "You were going to tell me about Marie," he said.

"Oh yeah. Marie and I were in the eighth grade when Dad quit drinking. Did you know she used to be really smart? She was the smartest kid in school. They wanted her to jump a grade, but around the same time Dad quit drinking, she got stupid."

"I don't think she's stupid," Shayne said softly.

"I don't mean stupid like *stupid*. I mean she just quit using her brain for, you know, *thinking*. She started hanging out with all these losers and getting high all the time. Her first boyfriend was Kevin Ungar. He got sent up last year for stealing a car. Then Derek Wilkes, who got stupid-drunk and crashed his car into the back of a cop car. His parents moved to some other state. And now she's with Jon."

Shayne was staring off into the distance. "Everybody makes mistakes."

"Believe me, you do not want to be one of Marie's mistakes."

"It doesn't matter. I'm not going to be around much longer."

"Where are you going?"

"I don't know. All I know is that sometimes bad things

happen and I have to do something about it, and every time I try to fix things they break even worse but I can't stop trying."

"You gave Marie a ride home last night," I said.

"Yeah."

"Notice anything different about her?"

"She seemed kind of hyper."

"Meth will do that."

Shayne drained the last of his coffee. "Meth? Marie is doing meth?"

"She thinks her ankles are fat."

"That's not good," he said.

"Nobody wants fat ankles."

Neither of us smiled.

"You know what we should do?" I said.

"What?"

"Go to my house so I can change out of this dink suit. And play some checkers."

"Why?"

"It helps me think."

Playing checkers did not help me think, but it did help me not think. Shayne and I were on our third game—I beat him every time—when I heard a motorcycle pull up in front of the house.

"Sounds like Marie's decided to come home," I said.

Shayne went to the window and looked outside.

"It's Trey," he said. "Alone."

"What's he doing here?"

Trey just sat there, as if trying to make up his mind about something.

"I'm going out to talk to him," Shayne said.

I followed Shayne outside. He glided up to Trey in that loose-limbed, ready-for-anything way he had.

"Hey," said Shayne.

Trey took off his helmet. "Hey."

"What's going on?" Shayne asked.

Trey said, "Marie's up at Jon's."

"We know that," I said. "So what?"

Trey seemed to notice me for the first time.

"Where's your suit?" he asked.

I had changed into a T-shirt and jeans.

"That's just for school," I said.

"You look almost normal. Only smaller."

"You look normal too, Trey. Only stupider."

Trey's eyebrows came together and I thought maybe I'd gone too far.

"What about Marie?" Shayne asked. "Is she okay?"

"Depends on what you mean by *okay*," Trey said, still looking at me.

"He means, is she *okay*," I said.

Trey's eyes got smaller, then he jerked his chin to the side, as if throwing off my words, as if what I said didn't matter because I was . . . *smaller.* He returned his attention to Shayne.

"This morning Wart and his girlfriend rode down to Hogfest, this big motorcycle rally, and left Jon in charge. It's been nonstop party central ever since. They're all tweaking."

"Tweaking?" I said.

"Yeah, doing meth. I mean, I'm wired enough already. But those guys, they smoke up and then take a bunch of Ativan to smooth themselves out, and then smoke up again."

"What about Marie?" Shayne asked.

"Her too." He rolled his massive shoulders in what I took to be a shrug. "Jon's kind of—well, you know how he is. Marie and him got in some stupid argument and he started slapping her around. I tried to get him to cut it out, but he went all postal on me and told me to get the hell out. When I left, Marie was in the bathroom with a bloody nose or something. Marie's nice. I mean, she was always nice to me, so I was thinking I should tell somebody."

Shayne was on his bike before Trey finished his sentence. We watched him tear off down the street.

Trey said, "Wow."

"Let's go," I said.

"Go?"

"Yeah. Take me there."

Trey looked down at me. "Mikey . . ."

I climbed onto his bike behind him.

Trey looked back at me. For a second I thought he was going to throw me off, but instead he shoved his helmet onto my head, started his bike, and we took off after Shayne.

35. THE INTERVIEW ROOM

"When was this?"

"Just a few hours ago."

"I thought Trey was the kid who tipped your bike over," Rawls said.

"Yeah. But like I told you, it was never his idea."

"Okay, so you went over to Wart's apartment because of what Trey told you . . ."

"Yeah, I went in the lobby and started punching call buttons until I got somebody who buzzed the door for me, then went up to the fourth floor. I knocked on the door to Wart's apartment, but nobody answered. I figured they were all up on the roof, but the roof access—one of those heavy-duty fire doors—was locked. So I kicked in Wart's door—"

"You kicked in the door?" Rawls looked at Shayne, who probably weighed less than the door.

"Yeah. The door wasn't all that solid." Seeing the expression on Rawls's face, he added, "It's a martial arts thing. Like breaking a brick."

"Oh, well then . . ." Rawls decided to file that with the other things he wasn't sure he believed. "Go on."

"Inside it was a nice apartment, but a real mess. Beer

bottles and pizza boxes everywhere. The apartment filled the entire top floor of the building—I think there were eight or ten rooms. There was a vintage Harley parked in the front room, like a piece of furniture. Three bedrooms, and some workrooms way in back. He's got quite an operation. You'd find it interesting."

"Was the girl there?" Rawls asked.

"No, everybody was up on the roof. It took me a while to figure out how to get up there, but I finally found a pull-down ladder in one of the closets. It looked like Wart cut through the closet ceiling and put a hatch in for his own private roof access. The hatch was open, so I climbed up and stuck my head out.

"The first thing I saw was Kyle, standing on this low wall at the edge of the roof, walking along it with his arms out like a tightrope walker. Tracy was yelling at him to get down; Jon was sitting on a sofa, laughing."

"There was a sofa on the roof?"

"Two of them, and some chairs, too. He had it set up like a living room with no ceiling. I climbed up out of the hatch. Everybody was watching Kyle. I just stood there, checking things out, waiting for them to notice me. I didn't see Marie at first. Tracy was standing there yelling at Kyle, Maura Dansky was curled up in one of those big club chairs. Tracy said if Kyle didn't stop screwing around, she was leaving. Kyle thought that was hilarious; he was laughing so hard I thought he was going to fall off the wall. Then Tracy went over to Maura and grabbed her, saying, 'C'mon, we're leaving.' Maura looked like she was drunk, but she let Tracy pull her out of the chair and across the roof toward the hatch. That was when they saw me standing there, and everybody froze.

"I stepped aside so that Tracy and Maura could get to the ladder. I told them—Maura and Tracy—to go. I think I said something like 'Party's over.' They looked back at Jon, then at me.

"Jon said, 'Party's not over until I say so.' But the girls were already climbing down the ladder. I walked toward Jon. That was when I saw Marie on the other sofa. I couldn't see her before because the sofa back was toward me. She was just lying there with her nose all swollen and her eyes closed.

"I said, 'Marie?' She didn't move. She was so still that, for a second, I thought she was dead, then she moaned and moved her arm a little.

"'She's having a little nap,' Jon said.

"I told him I was taking her home, but he said, 'I don't think so.'

"That was when he brought out the stun gun."

We were standing in the foyer trying to figure out how to get in when Tracy and Maura came out. Tracy was all jittery and brittle; Maura looked half-asleep.

"Party breaking up already?" Trey asked.

Tracy rolled her eyes and said, "Jon and Kyle are being stupid." She looked at me. "Your friend is up there."

"What about my sister?" I asked.

"She's there too." She went outside, dragging Maura with her.

Trey was holding the door open. "You sure you want to do this?"

"Not really." I stepped through the door and looked back. "You coming?"

Trey rolled his shoulders and followed me up the stairs. It was strange being with him, just like grade school all over again. And even though I was not completely sure whose side he was on, it felt good to have him there. Especially when we saw what had happened to the door of Wart's apartment.

"Jeez," Trey said, staring at the wreckage. The door looked as if someone had taken a battering ram to it. We entered the apartment not knowing what to expect.

Nobody was home.

"They're probably up on the roof," Trey said. He led me down a hallway to a closet. The closet door was open, revealing a steel ladder leading up to an open hatch, blue sky above. I could hear voices. Trey and I looked at each other. "You first," he said.

What I saw when I poked my head up through the hatch looked like a frozen moment in a video game. Shayne was standing with his back to me. About fifteen feet in front of him, Jon was sitting on a ratty sofa holding his stun gun. Over to my right, Kyle Ness stood on the edge of the roof, up on this low wall about two feet high. I pulled myself up onto the roof and stepped aside so that Trey could come up. I didn't see Marie at first, then I noticed her feet sticking out from the end of a second sofa.

Jon's eyes moved from Shayne to me.

"Hey, Mikey! It must be Wednesday!" He saw Trey clambering up to stand beside me. "Trey, my man! Where'd you disappear to?"

Shayne was standing very still, but even from the back I could tell he was on hyperalert. Jon stood up and took a few steps toward Shayne, pointing the stun gun at him. Then several things happened at once.

Jon pressed the trigger on the stun gun; there was a popping sound. Shayne moved impossibly fast, turning his body sideways to present a smaller target. Time slowed. I could see the darts leave the gun, like slow motion in an action movie. Shayne arched his back and the darts whizzed past him, missing by millimeters. I heard a strangled gasp from behind me. Both darts were sticking out of Trey's chest.

Trey's legs folded and he fell back through the hatch, thumping down the ladder.

Shayne was facing Jon again. Jon was frantically trying to pull the spent cartridge off the stun gun. I remembered from my own experience that once the dart cartridge was removed, the gun could still deliver a direct contact shock. Shayne saw what he was doing and started toward him, but Kyle had jumped from the wall onto the roof and was moving to intercept Shayne. He had something in his hand. The short, razor-sharp blade of his utility knife glinted. I shouted—I have no idea what I said. Maybe it was a scream. Shayne saw Kyle coming at him from the side and reacted, grabbing and twisting Kyle's wrist. The knife clattered to the rooftop. Shayne swung Kyle by his arm and hurled him at Jon, knocking both of them back onto the sofa.

Kyle was back on his feet in a second and went after Shayne again. His long arm shot out, his fist aimed at Shayne's head. With a movement that seemed almost casual, Shayne deflected the blow with his left hand, then drove his fist hard into Kyle's jaw.

Kyle's teeth clacked together; his head snapped back. Shayne instantly moved in and hit him twice more, once on each side of his face. Kyle dropped to his knees, tipped onto his side, and lay still.

During the three seconds it took for Shayne to flatten Kyle, Jon had pulled the dart cartridge off the stun gun and was on his feet, holding the gun in front of himself with both hands.

Shayne, about six feet in front of him, stood with his

hands at his sides, looking like a gunslinger from the Old West, waiting for the other guy to draw.

Jon triggered the stun gun, producing a blue electric crackle. Shayne didn't flinch. The gun would have to be pressed against his body for it to work, and he knew it. Jon edged to his right, away from the sofa. Shayne rotated slowly, following Jon, keeping the distance between them the same.

At that moment I felt the thrill of victory. Jon had the weapon, but Shayne was too smart, too fast. He had moves like a ninja and the confidence of one who knows he's in control.

Jon sensed that too—he wasn't smiling anymore. He backed away slowly, toward the edge. Shayne stayed with him, looking for an opening, waiting for Jon to make his move. I stood rooted to the spot; I think I was holding my breath. Then I noticed Kyle. He hadn't moved, but his eyes were following Shayne, waiting for his chance. Jon was forcing Shayne to turn his back on Kyle.

I yelled, but Kyle was already in motion. He rolled to his feet, grabbed the utility knife from where it had fallen, and launched himself cat-fast and rattlesnake-low at Shayne.

Shayne realized too late what was happening. Kyle buried the razor sharp tip of the knife in Shayne's calf. Shayne jerked his leg away from Kyle, whirled, and kicked. The knife flew from his calf, followed by a spray of blood droplets, and the heel of his cowboy boot struck Kyle on the side of his head with a sickening *thunk*. Kyle went down hard, but he had given Jon his opening. Jon lunged forward and jammed the stun gun into the small of Shayne's back. Shayne's body arched and he fell forward onto his face.

That was when my paralysis broke, or, as my dad might have said back in his drinking days, I *manned up*. It wasn't that I became courageous or brave; it was more like I had stepped outside my body and was watching myself running across the roof, straight at Jon. He saw me out of the corner of his eye, turned, and met my charge with a very large fist to my temple. My brain exploded and everything went dark gray. I didn't even feel myself fall.

I don't think I was out for more than a couple of seconds. When I came to, Shayne was a few yards away, close to the wall, his pant leg soaked with blood, trying to climb to his hands and knees. Jon, holding the stun gun, stood over him, once again wearing his terrible grin. I made a sound—more of a croak than an actual word. Jon looked over at me. Shayne tried to drag himself away, but Jon was too fast; he jammed the stun gun into Shayne's bleeding leg and held it there. Shayne convulsed, let out a ragged gasp, and collapsed again.

I staggered to my feet and ran at Jon again. I was beyond caring what happened to me. All I could see was that white grin shining out from a dark Jon-shaped silhouette, framed by sky. I'm sure he would have flattened me again, but Shayne reached out and swung his hand weakly against Jon's ankle. Startled, Jon looked down at Shayne. I threw myself at him, all 107 pounds of me, and hit him in the belly with both fists. Jon let out an *oof*.

He stumbled back, tripping over Shayne. The back of his knees hit the low wall at the edge of the roof and he sat down, dropping the stun gun to grab the wall with both hands.

I snatched up the stun gun and pressed it to his chest.

He laughed in my face.

I pressed the trigger and held it. The gun crackled. Jon's arms went slack. He wavered, then tipped slowly back.

There was a moment—maybe one second, maybe three—when I could have let up on the stun gun trigger. A moment when I could have grabbed him and pulled him back. A moment when I could have saved him.

But I didn't.

His feet came up off the asphalt roof. I remember seeing a bunch of tiny white roofing pebbles stuck in the black tread of his sneakers—and then he was gone.

He never even screamed.

A soundless roar filled Rawls's ears. *This must be what it's like for the deaf to witness a freight train passing,* he thought. He realized he was not breathing. Had the kid reached the end of his story? Rawls took a breath and waited out the silent seconds, watching the boy's pale, almost delicate hands play with the empty soda can, pressing in on the crumpled aluminum.

Rawls cleared his throat. "Let me see if I have this right. You got in a fight with these two, Jon Brande and Kyle Ness, and you knocked one of them unconscious and threw the other one off the roof?"

"Yeah."

"And nobody else was there? You were alone?"

"Marie was there, like I told you. But she was unconscious."

Rawls closed his eyes, then opened them. "Why would you tell me this?" he asked.

"What do you mean?"

"I mean, there was nobody there to see what happened. Why come here and tell me? Why not just say Jon fell, or jumped?"

"Because he didn't."

Rawls did not speak.

"Also, I didn't want somebody else to get blamed."

"Like who?"

"Anybody."

"What about the other kid, the one you knocked out?"

"Kyle was okay. He was breathing. I didn't hit him that hard. I took Marie to the hospital. She's there now. Then I rode around for a while. Then I came here." Shayne looked up. "Do you think I could get another soda? Mountain Dew's okay. Anything but cola."

"Sure." Rawls's voice came out husky. He cleared his throat. "Um . . . I suppose I should advise you of your rights. . . ."

"You mean like the right to remain silent? Too late for that." For the first time, Rawls saw the kid smile. Even after all he had just heard, Rawls still saw him as a boy, a half step beyond playing with his G.I. Joe. He reached into his pocket, came out with a cell phone, set it on the table. "There are some pictures on here you might like to look at."

"Let me get you that soda," Rawls said. "Then we can look at your pictures and talk about you making a formal statement. For the record."

Rawls's knees cracked as he pushed himself up from the table. He left the interview room, walked down the hall, took out his cell, and called downtown.

"First precinct," said the voice on the other end.

"Let me talk to Joe Spinoza," Rawls said.

Joe picked up right away. "Spinoza."

"Joe, this is George Rawls over at the Third. Listen, you have any incidents this afternoon? Anybody falling off a building?"

"What, are you psychic? Hell yes, we had an incident. Let me tell you. . . ."

Rawls listened, nodding. After a time he said, "Thanks, Joe."

"Tell me what you got," Spinoza said.

"I'll call you back." Rawls clicked off, closed his eyes, and waited for his thoughts to settle. He went down the hall to the vending machines. It was quiet in the station. No citizens waiting on the bench. Kramoski was sitting behind the high desk reading a book. Rawls looked at his watch. Six forty-five. The kid had walked in less than two hours ago, and Rawls felt as if he'd aged ten years.

As he fed a dollar bill into the soda machine, he thought about Shayne Blank's future. The court system would chew him up. He'd probably be charged with manslaughter, maybe worse. Even with a good lawyer he'd be doing time, rubbing shoulders with several hundred Jon Brandes. Long enough for him to learn how to jack cars and use a variety of illicit drugs and, basically, become a criminal. And then what? He shook his head. It wasn't fair. It was never fair, but it was what it was. He'd become a cop because he'd turned out to be a lousy teacher—like an untalented carpenter going into the demolition business.

But this kid . . . he'd never met one like this before. He walked slowly back toward the interview room, his thoughts running in hapless circles, and didn't notice until he was there that the can of soda in his hand was a Pepsi. He stepped into the room, his mouth poised to apologize for his selection.

He stopped, his mouth open.

The room was empty. Nothing but an empty soda can on the table, slightly crumpled, and a cell phone.

I dropped the stun gun. It hit the edge of the wall, wobbled for a moment, then slid over the side and fell. I leaned over and watched it clang off the fire escape railing, then continue falling.

"Mikey . . ."

I looked back. Shayne was sitting up, his face white.

"Are you okay?" he asked.

I felt the side of my head where Jon had hit me. It hurt, but it wasn't bleeding or anything.

"I think so," I said.

"What did you *do*?"

I leaned over the edge and looked straight down into the courtyard.

"He landed in the swimming pool," I said.

"Is he okay?"

"Somebody must have drained the pool," I said.

He climbed to his feet and looked over the edge. Jon was spread-eagled in the empty swimming pool, surrounded by a corona of blood. We stared down at him, rendered speechless by the enormity of what we—what *I*—had done.

Shayne said, "Marie." He ran back to where my sister

was sprawled on the sofa. Her face looked awful, her nose all swollen and discolored, but her eyes were half-open and she was trying to sit up. Shayne grasped her shoulders. Marie groaned and swatted his hands away.

"Lemme alone," she muttered.

Shayne helped her sit up. He kept talking to her as I stood watching, not knowing what to do. I felt as if I was smothering inside a fuzzy, invisible cocoon. I wondered if I was dreaming. Shayne walked Marie back and forth—Shayne limping and bleeding, Marie dragging her feet drunkenly. After a minute or two he sat her back on the sofa, then went over to Kyle and held a hand to his neck, checking for a pulse.

"He'll be okay," Shayne said after a few seconds. "Check on Trey. But don't tell him anything."

I looked down the hatch. No Trey. I climbed down. Trey had dragged himself out of the closet into the hallway. He was propped against the wall, holding his arm.

"I think it's busted," he said.

"We'll get you to a hospital," I said.

"What happened up there?" he asked.

"Nothing," I said. Everything, even the words coming out of my mouth, felt distant and unreal. I told my body to do things, and it responded.

Back on the roof, Shayne was kneeling in front of Marie, holding her wrists and talking to her in a low, intent voice. Marie nodded blearily, shook her head, winced. Shayne looked up at me. He stood up—I could see it hurt him—and came over to me.

"Is Trey all right?"

"He says his arm is broke."

"Can he walk, do you think?"

"He's pretty tough."

"Good. We have to get him and Marie out of here. Both of them need to go to the hospital." He put his hands on my shoulders. "Now listen to me, Mikey. This is important. You were never here. You and Trey. Never. Here."

I nodded numbly.

"I want you to keep your mouth shut, no matter what. Don't tell anybody anything. Will you promise me that? Not even Trey. Not Marie."

"What about you?" I asked.

"That doesn't matter. Mikey, are you hearing me?"

"I hear you." I felt absurdly grateful to Shayne for telling me what to do.

We got Marie down the ladder, listening to her woozy complaints all the way. When we got down, Shayne checked Trey's arm.

"It's broken," he said.

Trey managed a weak laugh. "Tell me something I don't know."

Shayne then gave Trey the same talk he'd given me. Trey listened, his face chalk-white, nodding at all the right moments.

By the time we left the apartment, Marie had recovered enough to walk on her own. Trey was on his feet too, though from the look of agony on his face it must have taken everything he had. Shayne improvised a sling out of a towel and tied it around Trey's neck and arm.

"There's a hospital a few blocks away," he said. "Do you think you can walk it?"

Trey closed his eyes and swallowed. "I think so," he said.

"Don't forget—you fell off your bike. That's all you tell them."

Trey nodded miserably. We took the elevator down, none of us speaking. Shayne got Marie on the back of his bike and took off with her. Trey and I made our way slowly toward the hospital. Several times, Trey had to stop and lean against a lamp pole or the side of a building—I thought for sure he would pass out, but he didn't.

When we got to the emergency room we found Marie slumped miserably in an orange plastic chair holding an ice pack to her nose.

"Where's Shayne?" I asked her.

She pointed at the exit.

I ran to the door and out onto the street. Shayne was on his bike, pulling away from the curb.

"Shayne!" I shouted as loud as I could.

He looked back and pulled over to the curb. I ran up to him. "Where are you going?"

"I have to do some things," he said. "You should go home."

"But . . . what about Marie?"

"Look, you can't be here. You were never here. I talked to Marie. She knows not to say anything."

I didn't understand.

Shayne smiled. It was a sad, ancient smile. I felt like a child.

He said, "Mike, I have to go now. It's time."

A cold, lost feeling rose up inside me. "No," I said.

"Yes," said Shayne. "You and your sister will be fine. Just go home."

"Where are you going?" I asked again—even though I knew he wouldn't tell me.

He shook his head slowly and smiled that ancient smile, turned his head, put his bike in gear, and pulled out onto the street. I watched him grow smaller as he rode away. Then he was gone.

39. MIKEY

Jon Brande didn't die. I didn't find out until the next day. Somebody must have seen him fall and called 911, and they'd rushed him to the hospital. I remember when I was in the ER, waiting with Marie and Trey, some paramedics had rushed through with somebody on a gurney, but I didn't know it was Jon.

It seemed impossible, that a guy could fall four stories and live. One theory was that he'd landed on the diving board and bounced off. In any case, Jon was messed up bad—broken vertebrae, broken pelvis, cracked skull, and a bunch of internal injuries.

Trey, his arm in a splint, told me all that at school on Thursday.

"He might not ever walk again," Trey said.

"Is he conscious?"

"He's talking, but he doesn't remember anything. Nothing." Trey gave me a long, measuring look.

"Kyle's okay?"

"Yeah, but he's not talking. How is Marie doing?"

"She's fine. They sent her home last night. Her nose wasn't actually broken, but she looks awful. And I think she's grounded for life."

"I haven't seen Shayne today."

"Me neither." I was dying to talk to him, but he hadn't shown up at school. I'd tried to call him, but his phone just went to voice mail. I didn't even know where he lived.

All that day I felt like I was in two worlds—the world of school and the world inside my head. I couldn't shake the images. Even when I was talking to somebody, or pretending to listen in class, I kept seeing the pebble-studded soles of Jon's sneakers as he tipped back off the edge of the roof. I kept seeing Marie's battered face, and Jon's spread-eagled body flat and bloody on the bottom of that pool.

The funny thing was that I didn't feel *bad* about what I had done. That one or two seconds when I could have let go of the stun-gun trigger and pulled Jon back onto the roof . . . those seconds were gone forever. And if I had pulled him back, something even worse might have happened.

I have no regrets, I told myself as I walked home. I was so far inside myself that I hardly noticed the unfamiliar car parked in front of our house.

An unfamiliar voice called my name. "Mike Martin?"

I turned to look at the man in the car. I'd seen him someplace before.

"Are you Mikey?" he said.

"Maybe."

He crooked a finger. I took a few steps closer to the car and suddenly remembered where I knew him from. He was the cop who had busted me for Advil.

I was pretty sure this time it would be something worse than Advil possession.

"Can we talk for a minute?" he said.

"About what?"

"You know a boy named Shayne Blank?"

"I go to school with him."

"Seen him lately?"

"Not today," I said.

"How about yesterday afternoon?"

"I saw him at school."

He smiled, letting me know I was getting the answers right—so far. But it wouldn't be long before I had to start lying.

"Why don't you hop in?" he said.

"Do I have to?"

"Either that, or we could go inside and talk about it with your parents."

I walked up to the car and got in.

He said, "My name is George Rawls. You remember me, don't you?"

"Yeah. You're the Advil cop."

"Actually, I'm more of an everything cop, but I do a lot of work with young people."

"Oh."

"Do you know where he lives? Shayne Blank?"

I shook my head.

"But he's a friend of yours, right?"

"Yeah."

"It's important that I talk to him."

"About what?"

George Rawls took a few seconds before answering, then shrugged and said, "There was an incident yesterday afternoon. A boy fell off a building and was badly injured. I think maybe you know him. Jon Brande?"

"I know him."

"Your friend Shayne stopped by the station yesterday and told me he'd thrown Jon off the building."

I'm not sure what happened with my face then, but Rawls found it fascinating.

"You didn't know?"

I shook my head.

"Apparently, your sister was involved as well. I talked to her on the phone a couple of hours ago. She claims she doesn't remember much."

"What did she say?"

"That she and Jon and some other kids were partying, and she and Jon got in a fight, and he hit her. Then she took some sort of painkiller and fell asleep. The next thing she knew, Shayne Blank was taking her to the hospital. But here's what puzzles me. Shayne gave me his home address, but the address turned out to be a vacant lot. And when I checked with the school, they had the same address for him. Supposedly, he was living with his aunt, but as near as I can tell, there is no such person. Do you know anything about that?"

I had no problem looking utterly bewildered.

"I see," said Rawls. He reached into his pocket, came out with a cheap-looking cell phone, and turned it on. "Prepaid cell," he said. "Your friend left it with me. A parting gift." He worked the buttons for a few seconds, then held it up so I could see the image on the phone display. "There are several photos here. Do you know what this is?"

The photo showed a long bench covered with beakers and assorted other chemistry stuff.

"It looks like a chem lab," I said.

He showed me the next photo, the same bench from another angle, and then a shot of some shelves filled with assorted packages of cold medicines.

"I don't get it," I said.

"What you're looking at is a meth lab. Is your friend Shayne involved with drugs?"

"No!"

"Take a look at the rest of these photos." He cycled through about ten more shots. More of the meth lab, then a shot showing the door, then a hallway, then several more shots of the interior of an apartment, including a picture of the Harley parked in Wart's living room.

"That's Jon's brother's apartment," I said.

"Wart Hale? How do you know? Were you there?"

"The motorcycle in the living room," I said, thinking quickly. "Marie told me about it."

He nodded, accepting my lie, then folded the cell phone and put it into his pocket. "So Wart is cooking meth at home. Now *that* is interesting."

Wart Hale returned from the Hogfest motorcycle rally the next day and walked into his apartment to find it full of police in biohazard suits dismantling his meth lab. His arrest was the lead story on the evening news, along with a piece on Jon Brande, who the newscaster characterized as "another young victim of the crystal meth epidemic."

Both Marie and I had to talk to the police several more times. Marie stuck to her claim that she didn't know what had happened on the roof, and I stayed with my story, that I had never been there. I could tell that Detective Rawls didn't believe me, but after repeating the lie again and again, it got easier, almost as if I believed it myself.

Marie never asked me what had really happened that day, but every now and then I caught her looking at me with this odd expression on her face, as if she wasn't quite sure who I was. I'll always wonder if she had seen me send Jon off that roof.

Eventually, things settled down to a new normal. Marie started seeing Trey Worthington. Marie helped him with his homework, so he was around a lot. Our parents didn't care for him much at first, but Trey turned out to be a pretty nice guy with Jon out of the picture. Also, he was good to have around when something needed to be lifted, pounded, or dragged. He and Dad bonded one day while digging out the elm stump in the backyard. Trey with an ax was a fearsome sight to behold.

Kyle Ness tried to take over Jon's drug business, got busted a month later, and was sent to Saint Patrick's Reformatory for Youthful Offenders. Tracy, Maura, Carlos, and the other stoners found a new supplier; I was happy not to know who it was.

Shayne Blank disappeared, no one knew where.

I went over to Pépé and Mémé's one afternoon in May and, over a game of checkers, told Pépé everything that had happened. Except for the part where I sent Jon off the roof. I told Pépé that Jon had fallen. It felt bad, lying to Pépé, but I was pretty sure he would prefer it to the truth.

Pépé listened to the whole story without interrupting me once. When I finished by telling him how Shayne had just disappeared without a trace, he leaned forward and said in a low voice, so that Mémé couldn't hear him from the kitchen, "That is how it is with *djabs*." Then he winked.

The other thing that happened that spring was I got a growth spurt. Only about an inch—okay, three quarters of an inch—but enough so that I've grown out of all my bar mitzvah suits. I took them all back to Thriftway—all ten of them—and got forty-three dollars. Mrs. Jerdes said she was overstocked in munchkin sizes. She didn't say it that way, but that was what she meant.

It's just as well—being rid of the suits, I mean. Shayne was right. The suits were a way of distancing myself from people, a way of masking myself the same way Marie uses her makeup or the way Jon used his smile. And I never said this to Shayne, but he was masking too: dressing all in black and never telling people who he really was or where he came from.

A lot of people don't want other people to know who they are. I think that, secretly, most of us would rather be somebody else. Me, maybe life would be easier if I was taller, lighter-skinned, smarter, and nicer. The first three I can't do much about, but being nice is something I might be able to pull off. It's hard, though, when you are as good at being a wise-ass as I am. But I'm working on it. Because being sarcastic is a mask too.

Speaking of masks, I got a visit from George Rawls a few weeks later, and he wasn't wearing his suit. He stopped by the house dressed in baggy green shorts, scuffed-up Nikes, and a bright yellow Hawaiian shirt printed with giant hibiscus blossoms. He must have dressed himself in the dark.

Being sarcastic again. At least I didn't say it out loud.

"I almost didn't recognize you," I said. Nicely.

"Same goes for you," he said. "No suit?"

"I outgrew them. Where's yours?"

"I quit the police."

"Oh. So, this isn't another interrogation?"

"Not at all. I just thought you might like to know, I found out a few things about your friend Shayne."

My heart started thumping so loud I could hear it.

"Turns out his real name is Herman LaRose."

"*Herman?*"

Rawls laughed. "I guess you can't blame him for changing it."

I stood there on the front step trying to breathe, realizing that I had almost convinced myself that Shayne had never existed.

"I might never have found out who he was, except he mentioned once he'd been in Louisville, so I called some of the schools there. One of the assistant principals knew who I was talking about right away. Said Shayne was a good kid. Kind of quiet, though. Until one day he got in a fight and beat up a couple of his classmates, then disappeared. I've traced him to three other high schools since, always calling himself Shayne Blank, never staying more than a month or two. None of the addresses he gave to the schools panned out—I suspect he was living in vacant houses, homeless shelters, whatever he could find.

"He mentioned once that he had learned self-defense from his father, and that his folks were military, so I called a friend of mine in Army Intelligence and asked him to poke around, see if any of his hand-to-hand combat instructors was missing a teenage kid. He had an answer for me within a few days.

"Kind of a sad case, really. Herman's dad was Special Forces, spent time in Iraq, the first war. His wife—Herman's mother—died in childbirth. The dad returned to the states and became a hand-to-hand combat specialist teaching at Camp Lejeune, in North Carolina. That's mostly where Herman grew up. But the old man had a breakdown eighteen months ago. He's now in a military psychiatric institution. Paranoid schizophrenia brought on by post-traumatic stress disorder. Herman went to stay with an aunt in Texas after his dad's breakdown. He stayed there about a year, then busted some kid's kneecap and ran away."

"Why?" I asked.

"Apparently he thinks he's some sort of vigilante. Every school he's been at, he's had a run-in with somebody. Turns out that every kid he's had a problem with was always a problem himself. The one in Texas was a notorious bully. In Louisville the kids he beat up were implicated in setting fire to a synagogue. In Oklahoma City it was a guy who date-raped one of the girls in school—he hit that kid so hard he crushed his cheekbone and dislocated his jaw. And after each altercation, Shayne—I mean, Herman—disappeared the next day." Rawls shrugged. "My guess is that he's just as crazy as his old man. But you have to give him credit for wanting to continue his education."

"Are you going to have him arrested? For what happened with Jon?"

"I'm not a cop anymore. Even if I knew where he was—which I don't—it's none of my business. Fact is, I'm going back to teaching."

"If you're not a cop, how come you went to all that trouble to find out about him?"

"I was curious." Rawls stood there without speaking for what felt like a long time. He cleared his throat. "You know how sometimes you meet somebody, and afterward you just can't go back to being what you were?"

"Because it's like they're watching you," I said.

"Exactly. Or because whatever you do, you're thinking,

If so-and-so could see me now, what would he think? I still think about my old man that way, and he's been dead twenty years. Anyway, I got the feeling after talking to him, and to you, that he mattered to you. I thought you'd want to know about him."

"That he was real," I said.

Rawls smiled. "That too."

I spent most of that night writing a letter to Shayne, telling him thanks, and that we were all okay. I told him that Jon was permanently in a wheelchair, that Trey was going out with Marie, that I had given up on the suits, and that even though I was still the smallest kid in school, I was bigger than I'd been when he knew me. I told him a few other things I thought he might find interesting, like that Dad and I had started shooting baskets every night after dinner. It turned out that he'd always wanted to, but he thought I wanted him to leave me alone. Also, I wrote how Trey and I were helping Dad build that backyard fountain where the stump used to be. Five copper goldfish shooting water from their mouths. It was going to be amazingly cool.

And I told him that even though we were all doing well, we missed him.

I signed the letter and put it in an envelope with some pictures I'd taken of me and Marie and Dad and of the fountain we were building. I wrote, "Shayne Blank, aka Herman LaRose" on the front, but I left the address blank.

If I ever found out where he had gone, I would fill it in and send it to him.